"Your Date Will Be Here Any Moment."

Elena turned around to meet the man the dating service had picked for her. Her eyes widened when she saw Garrett standing there!

"Garrett, I can't believe—" She was so thrilled that she could barely speak. "This is so incredible!"

He looked incredible. He was starkly handsome in a black tuxedo that stretched across his broad shoulders and solid chest.

She wanted to ask him a zillion questions about his signing up with the dating service, but she was so flustered being with him that she couldn't remember the name of the service.

Garrett slipped his hand in hers and led her to the dinner table. As he sat across from her, her heartbeat raced when she felt his knees touch hers.

"To us," he said, tapping her sparkling glass with his.

She nodded, unable to believe that her dream of being with him had come true.

Dear Reader,

This month, Silhouette Desire celebrates sensuality. All six steamy novels perfectly describe those unique pleasures that gratify our senses, like *seeing* the lean body of a cowboy at work, *smelling* his earthy scent, *tasting* his kiss…and *hearing* him say, "I love you."

Feast your eyes on June's MAN OF THE MONTH, the tall, dark and incredibly handsome single father of four in beloved author Barbara Boswell's *That Marriageable Man!* In bestselling author Lass Small's continuing series, THE KEEPERS OF TEXAS, a feisty lady does her best to tame a reckless cowboy and he winds up unleashing *her* wild side in *The Hard-To-Tame Texan.* And a dating service guarantees delivery of a husband-to-be in *Non-Refundable Groom* by ultrasexy writer Patty Salier.

Plus, Modean Moon unfolds the rags-to-riches story of an honorable lawman who fulfills a sudden socialite's deepest secret desire in *Overnight Heiress.* In Catherine Lanigan's *Montana Bride,* a bachelor hero introduces love and passion to a beautiful virgin. And a rugged cowboy saves a jilted lady in *The Cowboy Who Came in From the Cold* by Pamela Macaluso.

These six passionate stories are sure to leave you tingling… and anticipating next month's sensuous selections. Enjoy!

Regards,

Melissa Senate

Melissa Senate
Senior Editor
Silhouette Books

Please address questions and book requests to:
Silhouette Reader Service
U.S.: 3010 Walden Ave., P.O. Box 1325, Buffalo, NY 14269
Canadian: P.O. Box 609, Fort Erie, Ont. L2A 5X3

PATTY SALIER
NON-REFUNDABLE GROOM

SILHOUETTE *Desire*®
Published by Silhouette Books
America's Publisher of Contemporary Romance

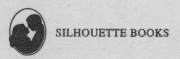 SILHOUETTE BOOKS

ISBN 0-373-76149-X

NON-REFUNDABLE GROOM

Copyright © 1998 by Patricia Bury Salier

This edition published by arrangement with Harlequin Books S.A.

® and TM are trademarks of Harlequin Books S.A., used under license. Trademarks indicated with ® are registered in the United States Patent and Trademark Office, the Canadian Trade Marks Office and in other countries.

Printed in U.S.A.

Books by Patty Salier

Silhouette Desire

The Sex Test #1032
The Honeymoon House #1091
The Love Twin #1121
Non-Refundable Groom #1149

PATTY SALIER

Born and raised in Gravesend, Brooklyn, in New York, Patty credits her mother for her keen logic and her father for her curious, creative mind. She has been a published writer for many years. To Patty, her wonderful husband and two great children are everything she could want in life. "I've got so much to be thankful for."

To my wonderful children,
Diana and Jeff

One

At Grant Property Management in Santa Monica, Elena Martin took a deep breath of courage as she stood up from her desk behind her office partition.

I'm going to get that promotion, she silently repeated like a mantra. *I've got to get that job!*

As she blindly grabbed the folders of the accounts she handled as a property manager, she anxiously thought of ways to convince her boss, Stanley Grant, that she was the perfect person to fill the now-empty seat of vice president.

Glancing down, Elena noticed that a button of her white silk blouse was open, revealing a peek of lacy white bra. She quickly tried to button her blouse and realized that the button hole had stretched too large to hold the button closed.

Everything's going wrong! she silently screamed.

Ever since she woke up that morning, her emotions had been in an uproar about getting the promotion. She'd left her wallet at home. She didn't even have her credit card to put gas in the near-empty tank of her car when she drove to work.

Realizing she was a couple of minutes late for her appointment with Stanley, Elena held the files in front of her chest, trying to hide the blouse button in case of another reopening. Then she headed toward his office, walking past the three junior property managers.

"Elena, wait," called out Grace, a woman in her early sixties who was the receptionist. "Stanley stepped out of his office for a few minutes."

Elena was too revved up with nervous energy to return to her desk. "He won't mind if I wait for him inside."

"But there's someone else—" Grace's voice trailed off.

The moment Elena entered Stanley's office, she came to a sudden halt.

"Stan, I—" a deep male voice began and then stopped.

He was standing by the window with a brown calf leather briefcase in hand. She instantly took in his curly black hair and six-foot, solid frame dressed in a gray suit, pressed white shirt and pale blue print tie.

"You're *definitely* not Stanley," the man said, his twinkling gaze appreciatively taking her all in.

His visual caress sent a tingle straight down to her toes. "I'm Elena Martin," she stammered, caught off guard by her sensual reaction to him. "I'm a property manager here at the Santa Monica branch."

His warm charcoal eyes held hers. "I've heard Stanley mention your name, but I can't believe I've never met you before," he said. "I'm Garrett Sims, a property manager at the Sherman Oaks branch." He stepped closer and extended his hand to her. She noticed that he wasn't wearing a wedding band.

His large hand covered hers, and she felt a jolt of electricity that completely overwhelmed her. She hadn't allowed herself to feel close to a man since what happened with her ex-boyfriend, Ted.

She quickly released her hand from his, trying to focus on her promotion goal. "I have a meeting with Stanley."

"So do I."

"Right now?"

"Well, yeah."

"That can't be," she said. "You must have your appointment time mixed up."

"I don't think so."

"I'm sure Stanley will explain your time confusion," she said.

"*My* time confusion?" he repeated with a warm twinkle in his eyes.

"That's right," she said, trying to ignore her strong attraction to him. She unconsciously set down her files on the coffee table. "You'll need to reschedule."

When Garrett didn't immediately respond, she noticed his gaze drift to her blouse. She looked down and saw that her button had reopened, and her bra was showing slightly.

She quickly grabbed the folders to her chest, feeling heat rise to her cheeks, not only from embarrassment, but from the spark of playfulness in his eyes that instantly turned her on.

Just then, Stanley walked in, rushed and preoccupied as usual. In his early sixties, he was stocky, graying and his face was always in a frown.

"I've got a lunch meeting right after this," Stanley said, sitting behind his desk, motioning them onto the sofa.

Superaware of Garrett beside her, Elena tried to ignore her ignited reaction to him.

"Stanley, could I talk to you alone?" she asked.

"Elena, I purposely scheduled you and Garrett together," her boss went on. "You want to be promoted to vice president, and so does Garrett. The problem is that I've only got one opening."

Elena's stomach tensed as she glanced at Garrett. She had to get that job. She desperately needed the salary raise to financially help out her younger sister, Jan, and Jan's two school-aged sons. Ever since Jan's husband had died of a sudden heart attack six months ago, her sister's job as a caregiver of elderly women had barely covered the bills. Jan's husband's small insurance policy had only covered the funeral costs and some unpaid bills.

She moved to the edge of the sofa. "Stanley, I'm very qualified for the position." Struggling to keep one folder against her blouse, she pulled out another folder. "On every expense report for the properties I manage, the budget is balanced. I've never exceeded the property owners' cap on expenses."

"Fine work, Elena," Stanley said, glancing at her expense reports, nodding, pleased. "You're doing an excellent job." He turned to Garrett. "Can I see your budget figures?"

Garrett glanced at her, and she thought she saw him hesitate before opening his briefcase. "Sure, Stan," he said, handing him a set of papers.

"Superb, Garrett," Stanley said, flipping through the sheets. "On every building you manage, the expenses are the lowest I've ever seen. You've saved our clients substantial sums of money. In fact, just today I received a call from one of our building owners praising your work."

Elena nervously bit the inside of her mouth. She could see Stanley leaning toward Garrett, and she didn't know what to do.

Stanley's telephone rang. "Excuse me." He took the call, swiveling the chair so his back was to them.

Garrett leaned closer to her. "Elena, if you want to talk separately to Stanley," he whispered, "I'll tell him I want that, too."

She could feel his warm breath against her hair. She could smell his musky aftershave. His sensitivity to her feelings surprised her, but she couldn't allow herself to focus on him if she wanted that job.

"Garrett, is the pressure of competing with me too much for you?" she daringly asked, needing to feel more in control.

His eyes held hers, almost in an embrace. "As a matter of fact, Elena, I'm thoroughly enjoying it."

So was she, but she didn't dare tell him!

"Garrett," she began, "I really need this job, and I'm going to get it!"

A grin spread across his handsome face. "Are you challenging me?"

"Well, yes," she replied, trying to keep her voice steady. "Yes, I am!"

His gaze remained steady on her. "I completely accept your challenge."

Her body grew heated at his words as she fantasized that he meant more than just the promotion.

Stanley hung up the phone. "You've both put me in a dilemma," he said, turning back to them. He pulled out a folder from a file cabinet. "I've got your résumés in front of me, and they're top-notch." He flipped through the paper. "Elena, your credits are very impressive. Three prior years of experience with Drexler Property Management, two years at my company. Now you're successfully managing ten properties for me."

She confidently glanced at Garrett with a silent, *I told you!* But when he smiled and nodded with genuine appreciation, she felt totally thrown off by him again.

"And you, Garrett," Stanley went on, sifting through the two-page résumé. "You've worked as a property manager for ten years, including three at my company. You're currently managing sixteen properties. And you've won the company award for Top Manager of the Year at the Sherman Oaks branch three times in a row.''

Elena suddenly felt ill. Garrett had tons of advantages over her. Experience, more accounts, company awards. *And* he was a man.

She knew that Stanley had only once hired a woman as vice president, and it was a disaster. She had learned from Grace that the woman fell in love with one of Stanley's property managers, abandoned the vice presidency to form a small company with her new husband and took most of Stanley's clients with her.

She was sure that Stanley wasn't eager to hire another female again. And Grace had told her that Stanley would never again promote or keep anyone who got romantically involved with a co-worker at his branch offices.

To get that promotion, she had to come up with a way to top Garrett's credits, and fast.

With a jolt of energy, she stood up and blurted, ''Stanley, I can prove I'm the perfect person for the job.''

Her boss's eyebrows lifted with interest. ''What do you propose?''

She could feel Garrett's eyes on her. She pressed the folder to her chest, trying to keep her mind focused on the job and not him.

''Give me one month, Stanley,'' she began. ''Besides doing my regular job, I'll rev up new accounts to increase your business.''

Stanley pulled his chair closer to his desk. ''Are you saying that you'll go out and get me new clients?''

''Absolutely!'' she blurted.

She panicked. She'd never gotten a new management account at her job. Elena had always been assigned properties to manage by Stanley. He was the one who got new accounts.

''Fascinating idea, Elena,'' Stanley said, pondering her concept.

"It sure is," Garrett added, looking at her, impressed. "How about if you and I compete for new accounts?"

"What do you mean?" she pushed out.

"The one who gets the most new clients for the company wins the vice presidency."

"Sounds fair to me," Stanley commented.

"I'm in," she responded, wanting Garrett to know she was ready to take him on full-force.

"Terrific," Stanley said. "Now my choice will be an obvious one."

Just as Stanley's phone rang again, Grace stuck her head in the office. "Elena, a tenant at the Fourth Street apartment building is having a problem and needs to speak to you."

"Thanks, Grace, I'll take it at my desk," she said, wishing she didn't have to leave at that moment. "I'll be right back."

As Stanley took his call, Garrett couldn't take his eyes off Elena leaving the office.

Her willful competitive nature turned him on. He was impressed that she wasn't intimidated by his longer experience at the company. He respected her headstrong desire to get the promotion over him at all costs.

The entire time she'd been in the office, Garrett could barely listen to Stanley talk about the promotion. He was totally mesmerized by her enticing blue eyes.

He yearned to run his fingers through her soft, shoulder-length, streaked blond hair. When he had caught a glimpse of the lace of her bra through her accidentally-opened button, he felt a moment of desire for her.

"Garrett, I like Elena's competitive-account idea," Stanley said, hanging up the phone.

"She's incredible," he said, and then quickly added, "I mean, she's a clever thinker."

"Garrett, I want to be very clear about one thing," his

employer went on. "What I said to you a few weeks ago still holds true."

"I haven't forgotten," Garrett said.

Stanley's proposal was etched permanently into his brain. He'd told Garrett that he planned to retire in the near future, but since he was a widower with no children to pass down the business to, he needed a good man to run his company.

Garrett's goal was to become that man. But first, he needed to earn the vice presidency and prove his abilities to govern the company.

"To be fair to Elena, I'm giving her idea an equitable chance," Stanley continued. "But I'll be honest. My eye is on you. I'm sure with your numerous contacts, you'll acquire plenty of new accounts to make my final decision an easy one."

"I won't disappoint you, Stan," he said firmly.

Yet, to his surprise, Garrett felt hesitant about power-housing for new accounts. And he knew why. He wished that Elena Martin wasn't his competition.

Stanley's phone rang again. Garrett saw Elena walking toward him. His body heat rose at the sight of her. He noticed that she'd safety-pinned her blouse, and the fabric strained across her full breasts. He'd never felt such a powerful reaction to a woman before—not even his ex-wife.

"Did I miss anything?" Elena asked him, her eyes taking in Stanley on the phone with his back to them.

"Stan's very impressed with your new account proposal," he said, feeling uneasy about his boss confiding that he favored him over her.

"I'm going to be vice president, Garrett," she boldly stated.

The fire in her eyes and the sensual way she was standing with her hand on her hip made him want to draw her into his arms and make wild love to her right then and there.

"Elena, have lunch with me," he said instead in a low voice so Stanley wouldn't hear.

"Lunch?" she asked, glancing worriedly at Stanley.

"I want to get a better sense of who my competition is."

He didn't know what was happening to him. He knew that Stanley was uncomfortable with employees romancing in the office. Yet when he was near her, he momentarily forgot his desire to become vice president. Being in her presence made him want to ignore every rule in the book.

"I can't have lunch with you," she told him.

Stanley hung up. "I'm off," he said, heading toward the door. "Good luck to the both of you."

The moment Stanley left, Elena nervously clasped her hands behind her back, superconscious of being alone with Garrett. Everything inside of her wanted to tell him yes for lunch. But how could she? She had just met him and already she was aching to spend more time with him.

Hadn't she learned from her last boyfriend, Ted, how rushing into a relationship spelled disaster for her? Besides, she knew that Stanley would never promote her if she got involved with one of his property managers.

Grace peeked into the office. "Elena, before you leave for lunch, your sister's on the phone."

"My sister?" Just being near him made her brain turn into mush. "Oh, sure, thanks."

"I could wait to go down in the elevator with you," Garrett suggested.

"You go ahead," she said. "I might be a while." She went to her cubicle.

Yet as she picked up the phone, she wanted to hurry so she could get to the elevator, hoping Garrett would still be there. She couldn't stop thinking about him!

Her sister sounded worried over the phone. "Mrs. Fowler's ill," Jan began, explaining that the elderly lady she cared for had to be taken to the doctor. "Tod and Bennie have a half day off from school," her sister went on. "Can you pick them up? I'll try to get home in a little while."

"Sure, don't worry," she told her. "I'll get the kids and meet you at your house."

She quickly hung up the phone, checking her bag to make sure that she hadn't forgotten Jan's house key like she'd forgotten her wallet at home. Relieved, she found the key and rushed out of the office into the hallway.

Her heart pounded when she spotted Garrett waiting for her. When he saw her, his eyes warmed, and a slow heat filtered through her body. The lunch crowd was pushing into the elevator.

He held open the door for her, even though the elevator was packed. Feeling trembly, she fit into the small space he made for her. She was facing him, and her body lightly pressed against his.

As the elevator vibrated going down, his hand gently brushed her waist to steady her. She felt the electricity of his touch through the fabric of her clothing.

She could feel her breathing quicken when his broad, hard chest lightly pressed against her breasts with the movement of the elevator.

The moment the parking garage level appeared, Elena quickly exited the elevator, slightly out of breath from her physical reaction to Garrett.

"See you," she said, hurrying to her car.

"There's still time to change your mind about lunch," he said.

She noticed him heading toward a blue Mustang parked next to her car. Her hand trembled as she put the key into the ignition, thinking about how much she wanted to have lunch with him.

She turned the key and the engine rolled over but wouldn't start. She tried again, but her car was dead. She stared at the empty gas gauge.

"Oh, no!" she said, panicking.

In the next moment Garrett was at her driver's window. "Car trouble?" he asked.

"I'm out of gas," she told him. "I promised my sister I'd pick up my two nephews from school."

"Come on," he said. "I'll give you a lift."

"I don't want to put you out."

He helped her out and then opened the passenger door of his car for her. "I'll consider it our lunch date," he said with teasing eyes.

As she slid into the front seat, she saw him take off his jacket and hurl it into the back. Her gaze lingered on the way his white shirt contoured his massive chest and muscular arms.

"Where to?" he asked, climbing into the driver's seat.

"Take a right on Florence Street," she replied, knowing she had to stop fantasizing about him.

"I'll get my mechanic to bring a couple of gallons of gas to the parking structure and fill your tank," he offered.

"You don't have to," she said, surprised.

"I want to."

She didn't know what to say. She was so used to handling her own problems and helping out her sister and nephews that she forgot what it was like to be taken care of.

"Do you live near your sister?" Garrett asked as he drove.

"My apartment's about ten to fifteen minutes away at One Hundred Rochester Drive." She abruptly stopped, realizing he hadn't asked for her address.

He glanced at her and smiled, as though he knew she'd given her address so he could ask her out.

"Are you at your sister's place a lot?" he pursued. "Or are you at home in the evenings and on weekends?"

"Most Saturdays and Sundays, I'm over at my sister's. I've been helping out ever since her husband passed away," she replied. "During the week, I usually work late hours."

"Every night?" His sexy eyes held hers. "Don't you set aside time for pleasure?"

"My life's too busy," she quickly replied, glancing away.

How could she tell him that she hadn't dated since her ex-boyfriend because she didn't know if she could ever trust a man's word again?

She spotted Van Dyke Elementary School up ahead. "There's my nephews' school."

Garrett parked his Mustang at the curb and watched Elena hurry out of the car toward the throng of laughing and chattering children.

He knew he'd upset her. Why had he asked such personal questions? He hadn't meant to. Yet, he couldn't help wanting to know everything about her.

"Bennie! Tod!" he heard her call out to two little boys, one taller than the other.

"Aunt Elena, where's Mom?" asked the little boy with the dirt-smudged face, who was running toward her with a backpack and a boxed juice in his hand.

As Garrett watched her give her nephew a warm hug, a feeling of sadness washed over him. A wife and children of his own were a dream he'd had a time ago. But not now, not after the trauma of his divorce. He knew that marriage didn't work for him.

"Aunt Elena, will Mom be home when we get there?" asked the older, taller boy, who seemed more mature and serious.

He heard her explain the situation as she took their hands and led them to his car.

"Garrett, I'd like you to meet Bennie," she began as they reached the car. "He's six years old and—"

"Smart!" Bennie spoke up for himself.

Garrett laughed. "How are you, Bennie?"

"And this is Tod," she went on. "He's nine and a fine baseball player."

"I'm a catcher!" Tod said proudly.

"Great position." Garrett shook his hand. "I'm a pitcher on a baseball team with my friends during my spare time."

"You are?" The older boy's eyes lit up. "Curve balls or windups?"

"Both," he replied. "Hop into the back, guys."

As he opened the door for Elena, she whispered, "You're great with kids."

"So are you," he told her, feeling an inner connection to her that he'd never felt with a woman before.

"Are you my aunt's new boyfriend?" Bennie asked, wide-eyed.

He noticed Elena's cheeks turn scarlet as he gunned the engine.

"Garrett works at the same company I do," she told him.

"Do you car pool to work together?" Bennie further inquired.

"I don't even know where Garrett lives," she said, her blue eyes on him.

"My apartment is in Santa Monica," he told her.

"We live so close," she said.

Thoughts of asking her out rushed into his brain, but he squashed them down, knowing she deserved more than he could give her.

"Where do you play baseball, Garrett?" Tod asked, picking up Garrett's mitt from the back seat of the car.

"During the week, I practice at night at the Santa Monica baseball field," he replied. "Where do you play, Tod?"

"At the Westside Little League field," he said proudly and then added in a voice for only him to hear. "Maybe you can come with Aunt Elena and see me play sometime."

He glanced at Elena, wanting to say he would so he could be with her again. But he knew that he could never get that deeply involved in her life.

"My sister's house is two blocks down," she told him, interrupting his thoughts.

"Sure thing," he said, suddenly conscious of their ride being almost over and not wanting to leave her.

He parked the car, and just as he pulled the front seat forward for the kids to get out, Bennie popped the straw out of his boxed juice. Dark purple liquid shot straight onto Garrett's snowy-white shirt and clean tie.

"Oh, no, Bennie!" Elena called out. "Garrett, I'm so sorry!"

"It's okay, really," he said. "I'll drop by my apartment to change before I go to my appointment."

"Appointment?" she repeated, horrified. "Maybe you'd better come inside. I'll wash out the stains by hand and throw your shirt in the dryer. It'll only take a few minutes."

As she unlocked the front door, Garrett knew he should thank her and leave. He realized that entering her sister's house would personalize his relationship with her even more. Yet he felt drawn to her in a way that he couldn't resist.

Elena led Garrett into Jan's kitchen while her nephews ran into the living room to play. She couldn't believe she'd invited him inside. She kept telling herself that she felt responsible for his soiled shirt. Yet she knew her invitation meant a lot more to her than that.

"The washer and dryer are in here," she told him, turning on the light of the tiny, narrow laundry room.

As she went in, she felt Garrett's body close to hers. "Give me your shirt," she said, "and I'll clean off the spots."

He undid his stained tie and put it on the supply shelf. As he pulled off his shirt, she was superaware of his muscular, bronzed chest and shoulders. She felt the impulse to glide her palms across his bare skin and press her lips...

She quickly turned on the faucet in the sink, hoping he couldn't see how turned on she was just being near him. She tried to concentrate on rubbing the stain remover into the spots, but all she could think about was his powerful frame only inches from her.

As she put his shirt in the dryer and turned on the knob, she felt his finger gently push a strand of hair from her eyes.

"You're a beautiful woman, Elena," he said.

She looked up at him, feeling the tenderness of his words. His gaze drifted to her lips. As his mouth neared hers, she saw the laundry room door closing. The lock clicked shut, and the lights went out. Against the whizzing of the dryer, she could hear Bennie giggling outside the door.

"Bennie!" she called out, remembering she'd scolded him the last time he'd locked the door when she was inside.

"Aunt Elena, let's play hide and seek with Garrett!" he called out.

"We can't play now." Her breathing quickened when she felt Garrett tenderly touch her cheek with the side of his thumb. "Bennie, please open the door."

"I can't! I've gotta go to the bathroom!" Then she heard him run out of the kitchen.

Alone with Garrett in the darkness, her heart thumped against her ribs. She felt his hand slip around her waist and draw her against his bare chest. His lips touched her earlobe, his warm breath on her neck. As his mouth closed over hers, she parted her lips, wanting to feel closer to him.

Just then Tod's voice bellowed outside the door. "Bennie, why did you lock in Aunt Elena and her friend? That was dumb!"

"*You're* dumb!" Bennie shot back.

In the next instant the lock released. The door swung open, and the laundry room lights flashed on. She quickly broke free of Garrett's arms. Her skin was burning hot. She could barely catch her breath.

As her nephews chased after each other out of the kitchen, she pulled out Garrett's shirt from the dryer, avoiding his eyes.

"I can iron it, if you want," she said in a shaky voice.

He touched her hand. "Elena, I shouldn't have—"

"The stains are out," she told him, aching to be in his arms again. "My sister should be home any minute. She can drive me back to work."

"I can wait and take you myself," he said.

"I'll be okay," she said. "Thanks for everything." She wanted to tell him that she didn't want him to leave. She wanted to be locked in the laundry room with him all over again.

"Sure, anytime," he said, slipping on his shirt as he headed out of the laundry room. "See you, Tod and Bennie!" Then she heard the front door close.

Elena leaned against the dryer, feeling weak in the knees. Why had she allowed herself to fall into Garrett's arms? She could easily give her heart and soul to Garrett, only to end up finding out that he had zero interest in making a commitment.

Elena had already traveled on that painful highway with her ex-boyfriend, Ted. Her heart had been so caught up in Ted that she didn't see the warning signs.

She'd believed Ted when he said he couldn't see her on weekends because, as the partner of a bi-coastal law firm, he had to travel back and forth from Los Angeles to New York on business.

She had believed him when he said his Beverly Hills apartment wasn't warmly furnished like a home because he had no time to put into domestic matters.

She'd believed him when he whispered that he loved her and wanted to be with her forever.

Then, after dating him for eight months, he'd invited her to go on a weekend business conference in New York. She secretly believed he was planning to ask her to marry him.

However, in the hotel room, while Ted was in the shower, she answered the ringing telephone. She was devastated when she heard a woman's voice saying that she was Ted's wife and asking to speak to her husband.

Feeling used and deceived by the man she loved, she left the New York hotel room before Ted got out of the shower, and never saw him again.

Elena had convinced herself that she had no interest in getting seriously involved with a man again—until she met Garrett Sims.

He had made an impact on her the moment she met him in Stanley's office. Alone in the laundry room, she'd gotten so turned on by him that she'd momentarily forgotten he was competing with her for the job she wanted.

As she was about to walk out of the laundry room, she spotted Garrett's stained tie lying on the shelf. She held the silk in her hand, as though she was touching a part of him, knowing she had to forget her intimate moments with him and see him as her business competitor.

She heard Jan burst through the front door. "El, where's your car?" her sister called out.

In the kitchen she found her sister going through the

mail. Bennie and Tod ran in, gave their mother hugs and hurried back into the living room to play.

"I ran out of gas," Elena replied.

"How'd you get here?"

"I caught a ride with Garrett Sims," she quickly replied. "He works at Stanley's branch in Sherman Oaks."

"By any chance, is Garrett the owner of that tie?" Jan asked with great interest, still sorting through her mail.

She impulsively put the tie behind her back. "Bennie accidentally squirted juice on Garrett's shirt," she explained. "I washed out the stains and—" Her face heated up as the intimate memories rose in her mind.

"And what?" Jan pursued with a mischievous smile.

"We got locked in the laundry room together for a few seconds."

Her sister's eyes widened. "What happened next?"

"Okay, we kissed!"

"When are you going out with him?" Jan went on. "Is he sexy? How tall is he?"

"Jan, I can't have a relationship with Garrett," she said, frustrated. "He's off-limits for me."

"Why?"

"I'm competing with him for the vice presidency!"

"Oh, no."

"He's got tons more experience than I do," she rushed on, needing to share her upset. "And now, because of my insane idea, Stanley's going to choose one of us based on how many new accounts we can get for the company."

"El, what're you going to do?" Jan asked worriedly as she opened a large manila envelope.

"I need to stay as far away from Garrett Sims as I can," she replied, knowing how difficult that would be. "Stanley will completely eliminate me if he thinks I'm having an office romance with Garrett."

"You like him a lot, don't you?"

"He's different, Jan," she admitted. "I've never met a man like him before."

"And if the job wasn't in your way?"

All of her doubts about being in a serious relationship re-surfaced. "I wouldn't date him," she forced out.

"El, I know how worried you are about falling in love with a man who doesn't want to get married," Jan said. "But all of your worries are over."

"What do you mean?"

"I was a first-caller winner in a radio contest," she said, glancing at the document in her hand. "I just received my prize! Free enrollment in a dating service called the Marriage Connection!"

"The service is going to send you on dates?"

"Not me, silly," her sister said. "You!"

"What?"

"El, you're always doing stuff for me and the kids," she hurried on. "Now I get to pay you back. I gave your name to the dating service."

"You didn't!"

"This is the ideal way for you to connect with the right man for you," she explained. "Eighty percent of couples that have been matched by the Marriage Connection have ended up getting married!"

"Jan, I don't want to meet a man through a dating service," she protested, thinking about Garrett, wishing he could be that man for her.

"Just think—you don't have to worry anymore about being hurt by a guy who doesn't want to make a commitment," Jan went on. "The Marriage Connection only matches couples who sincerely want to get married." She showed her the document. "All you need to do is sign this two-page form agreeing to specific conditions."

Elena reluctantly read the first page of the form indicating that no real names, home or office addresses, or phone numbers are given until both parties have met.

Then her eyes landed on one particular sentence on the first page. "The only requirement is a commitment to want to get married."

Her heart ached to be with a man who truly desired a future with her—a man like Garrett. She quickly brushed her fantasy aside.

"What if the guy they pick out is totally wrong for me?" she asked.

"Look at the second page of the agreement," Jan encouraged.

She caught the sentence on the second sheet. "You are only required to go on three prearranged, already-paid-for dates, one every two weeks."

"El, just three dates," her sister pushed.

"I don't know."

"You can't say no," Jan told her. "I've already given your personality profile to the service, and you've been matched with a great guy, who you will be going on all three dates with."

"The dating service has already picked out a man for me?" She couldn't imagine meeting a guy more perfect for her than Garrett.

"The letter says that he has a successful career in real estate," Jan excitedly went on. "He's three years older than you, enjoys romantic dinners and walking on the beach under the moonlight. *And* he must sign the agreement stating that his goal is to get married. Perfect, right?"

Sure, if it was Garrett! she wanted to say but didn't. She couldn't spoil her sister's surprise gift to her.

"I'll think about it, okay, Jan?"

"There's no time," she said. "Your first prearranged date is set for this Saturday night."

"Saturday?" she repeated incredulously.

Before Jan could reply, Bennie ran into the kitchen

looking upset. "Mom, the words in my reading book are fuzzy looking."

"We need to get your eyes checked, Ben," her sister said, lovingly kissing him on his forehead. Then he went back to his activities.

Elena could hear the frustration in her sister's voice. She had no vision insurance to cover the cost and had been putting off making an appointment until she had the money.

"Jan, we're getting Bennie to an optometrist next week," Elena said.

"But I can't."

"We'll manage with the money," she reassured her, knowing more than ever how much she needed that raise.

"El, please let me pay you back with this dating service prize," her sister pleaded. "Sign the Marriage Connection agreement so I can feel like I'm giving you something in return."

Knowing how much it meant to her sister, Elena reluctantly put her ink signature at the bottom of the second page of the form.

After her sister dropped her off at the office parking structure to get her car, she realized that she still had Garrett's tie. She pressed the silk against her face, drawing in the musky scent of him.

Stop it! she scolded herself. *You can't think about him in a romantic way!*

As she got into her car, she started up the engine and saw the gas gauge arrow rise to mid-level. Garrett had taken care of her fuel problem, just as he promised. He was so incredible—considerate, kind, caring. Every quality he possessed was what she dreamed of in a man, except she needed to know one thing.

Did Garrett want a committed relationship like she did? She could never get deeply involved with a man again until she was sure he wanted a future with her.

As she zoomed out of the parking structure to a property management appointment in West Los Angeles, she kept reminding herself that getting the vice presidency was her priority, not Garrett Sims.

Then why did she drape Garrett's tie gently across her lap as if it was the most precious object in the world to her?

TWO

Garrett tried to concentrate on the traffic as he drove to the singles-only apartment building he managed in Palms. He could still smell the vanilla scent of Elena and the feel of her soft lips against his.

Everything about Elena captivated him. He admired how warm and gentle she was with her nephews. The nurturing way she took care of him made him feel so close to her, almost like he was part of her family.

In the laundry room he had been so turned on.... If the door hadn't burst open—

His foot suddenly hit the brake pedal when he realized he was about to rear-end the car in front of him.

What the heck am I thinking? he silently demanded. He couldn't allow himself to desire her. She was caring and giving and loving. She was definitely a marrying kind of woman. But he wasn't a marrying kind of man. He used to be. He used to dream of having a wife and children more than anything. After what happened in his past marriage, he had no intention of signing a marriage license again.

He never should've kissed Elena. He never should've touched her soft skin. But being near her made him want to cuddle and hold her body close to his.

As he drove and anxiously reached for his tie, he realized that he'd left it in the laundry room. He knew he should wait until tomorrow morning to call her about it. But the need to connect with her again was stronger than he wanted to admit.

As his car neared the two-story building in Palms, he picked up his car phone, dialed the Santa Monica branch and learned from Grace that Elena was out of the office. He quickly told Grace that he had business to discuss with Elena and got her cellular number.

He parked his car in front of the complex and dialed Elena's number. When he heard her velvet voice answer the phone, he was hooked all over again.

"Elena, I forgot my tie at your sister's," he began.

"I've got it with me," she said. "When I get back to the office, I'll send a messenger over to the Sherman Oaks branch."

"How about if I drop by and pick it up?" he suggested, wanting to see her again, even though he knew he shouldn't.

"Stanley might be here," she replied a bit nervously.

"Yeah, that could be a problem," he said, knowing he couldn't jeopardize their chances to the promotion. He felt the urge to ask if he could drop by her apartment to get it, but he didn't dare cross that boundary line.

"I could stop by after the office closes at seven tonight."

"I might be gone by then."

"I'll take the chance."

A few minutes later Garrett entered the lobby of the Palms apartment building.

"Garrett, just the man I want to see," said Sam McGrath, the middle-aged owner of the building.

"Hi, Sam, are there any problems with the pipe replacement job?" he asked, referring to the plumber who was replacing some of the old, leaky pipes.

"No further leaks yet," the owner replied. "Have you worked with this plumber before?"

"He's not my regular vendor," Garrett replied. "The plumber I usually deal with is ill. But I'll make sure the work goes smoothly."

"Garrett, your new apartment may become available very soon," Sam said.

"My new apartment?" he asked, confused.

"How could you forget?" Sam asked, surprised. "You signed the lease months ago and paid me the security deposit, plus the first and last months' rent to hold the place."

"Yes, of course," he said, realizing that he was so consumed with thoughts of Elena that he'd forgotten everything but her. "When will the apartment be ready?"

"The tenant in twenty-eight may be leaving for Florida earlier than he planned." Sam McGrath headed toward the front door of the lobby. "I'll let you know when the space is vacant."

"Thanks a lot, Sam."

As Garrett looked for the plumber, he waited for a rush of excitement to hit him, knowing he'd be moving sooner than scheduled into the apartment he'd been waiting for. Renting a place in the singles-only complex in Palms had been his goal ever since his divorce.

Garrett had been willing to do everything he could to keep the idea of getting married again permanently out of his brain.

He remembered when he'd met his ex-wife, Claire, a few short years ago. He'd just moved to Los Angeles from Seattle. He had no friends in L.A., just his elderly Aunt

Rosie and a good job opportunity at Grant Property Management.

He'd met Claire at a jazz club where she was waitressing. She'd instantly connected with him and became his friend, cohort and lover. After a few months of constantly seeing each other, he'd fallen in love. When she excitedly mentioned marriage, he didn't hesitate.

To Garrett, marriage was forever, a commitment to stay together for always. He believed that Claire felt the same way, too.

However, after six months as husband and wife, when he mentioned starting a family, she seemed preoccupied. She said her mother in Colorado was very ill and didn't have ample medical insurance to cover the bills. Responding to her need, he agreed that she should withdraw a huge chunk of savings from their account.

Before he realized it, she'd cleaned out their bank cash, maxed out their credit cards and borrowed a bundle of money from the bank.

The night he planned to talk to her about what was going on, he got home from work and found all of her belongings gone from their apartment. Distraught, he called a waitress friend of hers at the club. He was devastated to discover that she'd bought herself a brand-new red Camaro, packed all of her things and run off with a guy she'd met at the jazz club.

With a stack of creditors' letters in hand, Garrett went through the emotional trauma of the divorce. He realized that their marriage had meant nothing to her. *He* had meant nothing to her. She'd let him down, and no matter how hard he tried, he couldn't sustain a happy, satisfying marriage.

He remained at the apartment he'd shared with her, but every time he bumped into married neighbors, he was constantly reminded of how his marriage had failed.

He'd lucked out when he was given the singles-only

building to manage by Stanley and learned that the tenants signed a two-year lease agreeing to live a singles life while at the complex.

The moment he had heard that an apartment might become available in a few months, he had quickly signed the two-year lease and paid Sam McGrath a fistful of money ahead of time to guarantee his spot.

He needed to be alone. He couldn't imagine sharing his life again.

Garrett saw the plumber coming out of an apartment. He started down the hall toward him. As Garrett talked with the plumber, he realized how conflicted he now felt about moving into the singles-only building. Meeting beautiful, sexy, bold Elena Martin had totally jolted his world.

And, as he listened to the plumber, he kept glancing at his watch, wanting seven o'clock to roll around so he could be with Elena again.

At the office Elena nervously looked at the office wall clock. It was six forty-five. In fifteen minutes, Garrett would arrive to pick up his tie. She anxiously glanced at the extension phones on her desk and noted that Stanley's line was still lit. Everyone in the office had left, except him.

She held Garrett's tie in her hand, thinking of an excuse to leave before he arrived. She couldn't risk Stanley's seeing them together. Maybe she could set his tie on her desktop where he could find it. Why wasn't she doing it? She knew why. Because she couldn't wait to see him.

"Are you working late tonight, Elena?" Stanley called out, walking toward her partition.

She frantically jammed Garrett's tie into her top drawer. "I have some paperwork to finish," she replied, quickly shifting folders on her desk to look busy.

"One of these days I've got to cut down my late

hours," her boss said. "I go home almost every night with a headache and sometimes chest pain. I feel so tense sometimes."

As he continued talking, her stomach churned. Garrett would be there in a few minutes. Stanley would immediately be suspicious. She wished she'd insisted that Garrett not come. But her attraction to him had taken over, and now she might pay for it.

"Don't work too late, Elena," Stanley went on. "You'll wind up with ulcers like me."

"I plan to leave in a few minutes," she pushed out. Her eyes darted to the wall clock. Six fifty-five!

"Maybe I'll wait and ride down in the elevator with you," her employer said.

"Don't do that," she blurted. "I mean, you better go without me." She grabbed a stack of files. "I forgot that I've got tons of filing to do, too."

"Well, have a great evening," he added.

The moment Stanley was gone, she grabbed Garrett's tie out of the drawer and put it on top of her desk where he could easily find it. She was not going to take a chance like that with her boss again.

She waited a few minutes for Stanley to get into the elevator. Then she grabbed her bag, opened the front door and slammed straight into Garrett's arms.

Her heart pounded wildly in her chest at the feel of his warm hands on her shoulders. "Did Stanley see you come up in the elevator?" she anxiously asked.

"No," he replied. "And if he had, I planned to tell him that I came to see him. I wouldn't do anything to mess up your opportunity for the promotion, Elena."

His eyes held hers with a warmth and trust that made her melt inside. "I'll get your tie," she stammered.

At her desk, she was ultraconscious of his body so near hers. Her hand trembled a little as she handed him the tie.

"Are you sorry I came, Elena?" he asked as he took the tie.

"It was tense waiting for you," she told him. She couldn't tell him that she felt exhilarated being with him. Wouldn't that bind her closer to him before she knew what he was looking for in a relationship?

He gently slipped the tie around her neck and drew her close to him. "I had to see you," he admitted.

"I'm glad you're here," she heard herself say.

His gaze drifted to her lips, and she wanted him to kiss her more than anything. Then his mouth covered hers. When she felt his tongue touch hers, every vein in her body felt electrified. She lightly bit his bottom lip, and he moaned. Responding to his passion, she circled her arms around his neck and pressed her body tightly against his.

The ringing of the telephone suddenly brought her back to the office. She slipped free of his arms, handed him the tie and picked up the receiver. Her sister's voice filled her ear.

"El, why are you still at the office?" Jan asked. "You always let me know when you're working late."

"Sorry, I forgot to call," she told her, aware of Garrett's fingers lightly touching her hair. "I had some things to finish up."

"I received a card from the Marriage Connection," her sister went on. "It's got the name of the restaurant for your Saturday night date."

She saw Garrett walk over to the window. She felt guilty talking to her sister about a date with another man when she wanted to be with him. How could she go out on a date with someone else when her heart ached to be with Garrett?

"Jan, I'll talk to you later." Then she hung up and picked up her bag. "I've got to go," she said, avoiding his eyes because of the content of her sister's call.

In the hallway she was relieved when the elevator immediately came, and there were a few people inside as she got in with him. She blindly stared at the floor numbers lighting up on the metal wall.

The elevator doors opened at the parking level. As she was about to say a quick good-night to him and hurry to her car, he touched her arm.

"Will you be okay getting home?" he asked.

His caring made her feel even more upset about that date. "I'll be fine," she told him and then got into her car.

As she drove out of the parking garage behind his car, she watched him head up the street. She fantasized about blowing her horn to stop him and inviting him to her apartment. She wanted to know all about him. She wanted to cook dinner for him. She wanted to cuddle on the sofa with him.

Instead, she turned on a jazz station on the radio. She had to take her mind off Garrett. She couldn't be with him if he wasn't looking for a lifetime relationship like she was. Maybe the Marriage Connection date wasn't such a bad thing. Maybe meeting another man would steer her thoughts away from Garrett.

As she stopped for a red light, she heard him blow his horn and saw him wave as his car moved way ahead of hers up the street. She waved back and realized that no matter how hard she tried, she couldn't fight the growing inner connection she felt toward him.

As Garrett parked in front of Aunt Rosie's house, he waved to the young woman leaving, who took care of his aunt's needs from Monday through Friday. On Saturdays, a warm-hearted older woman came by.

Garrett unlocked the back kitchen door with his key. "Aunt Rosie, it's me!" he announced, entering the Early-American-style kitchen. He could hear the voice of her favorite radio talk show host from the living room.

"I'm catching the end of my show, Garrett," Aunt Rosie said. "Can you bring me a glass of grape juice?"

"You're allergic to grapes," he reminded her, pouring her a glass of orange juice instead. Though his aunt had lapses in memory and her eyesight was failing, she was as spunky as ever. As a widow with no children, she'd raised him since he was seven years old, when his parents gave her permanent custody due to their severe alcoholic drinking problem. Now that she was in her late seventies, he'd been caring for her by dropping by each day for a visit.

For the first time since his divorce, Garrett felt a pang of loneliness being at Aunt Rosie's house. He wished Elena was with him. Knowing how family oriented she was, he was sure she'd enjoy his aunt. He quickly shed the thought. He knew he could never introduce Elena to his aunt. He couldn't take the chance of getting that close to her. And he couldn't tell his aunt about her. Talking about Elena would mean that he envisioned her as the permanent woman in his life. Everything inside of him resisted making solid plans like that for himself again, knowing how easily his future with the woman he loved could be shattered.

When Garrett walked into the living room to give his aunt the orange juice, she immediately waved him to sit down and be quiet. He knew she didn't want him interrupting the remainder of the radio show.

He waited as she listened closely to every word of the host.

Aunt Rosie flipped off the radio. "Garrett, I got you a date for this Saturday night."

"With who?" He grinned, not taking her seriously. "Michelle Pfeiffer?"

"Ha, ha, very funny," she said. "Since you're not looking for a girlfriend yourself, I've decided to do it for you.'' She pointed to the coffee table. ''Hand me that sheet of paper over there.''

He felt the urge to tell her about Elena, but he didn't want her thinking he was serious with anyone. ''What's your plan for me, Aunt Rosie?''

''I heard about a dating service on the radio,'' she replied. ''It's called the something connection. I can't read the print too well, but the service chooses an ideal woman to match the man's personality. I paid the fee and sent a personality profile on you.''

''You're joking,'' he said.

''You need to sign this form,'' she said, handing it to him.

Garrett reluctantly looked at the paper. ''This is the second sheet to the agreement. Where's the first page?''

''It's around here someplace,'' she replied, sifting unsuccessfully through a stack of old newspapers on the floor. ''I think page one gave the name of the dating service and a couple of rules I can't remember.''

The idea of being with a woman other than Elena was making him more nervous by the second. ''Aunt Rosie, you're wonderful for thinking about me, but—''

She stuck a pen in his hand. ''You need to date a woman who's compatible with you,'' she went on. ''You made a big mistake with that con lady you married.''

Her words stung because he knew she was right. ''Okay, I admit, I should've listened to you about my ex-wife.'' His aunt didn't approve of her from day one. He couldn't help thinking that she'd like Elena.

''Sign this paper, Garrett,'' his aunt pushed. ''You might be matched with someone really nice.''

He couldn't envision meeting a woman more perfect than Elena. His impulse was to say no, but he stopped himself.

''I need to read the rules first,'' he said, knowing how

persistent his aunt could be when she felt strongly about something. He'd do anything for her, and she knew it.

He read that he'd only be obligated to go on three pre-arranged, already-paid-for dates, one every two weeks, beginning with the upcoming Saturday. He could feel his aunt looking over his shoulder, waiting for his signature on the form.

"Okay, three dates, that's it," he said, forcing himself to sign.

"Garrett, you need to promise me one thing," Aunt Rosie began. "Never tell your date I talked you into joining the service. That's no way to start a romance."

"I promise," he told her, making a mental note to write a check to cover the cost of the service and deposit the money into his aunt's bank account in the morning.

When he returned to his apartment in Santa Monica, Garrett felt uneasy about the prearranged date for Saturday night. Before he met Elena, he would've thought of the dates as three fun evenings, and that was it. But now he had no desire to go out with anyone, except her.

He shed his clothes and jumped into the shower, trying not to think about his powerful feelings for her. But when he flashed on holding her soft body in his arms at the office, he fantasized about what it would be like to hold her naked against him.

He turned on the cold water full-force. Temporarily dating a woman chosen by a service was a lot safer than being tempted by his intense attraction to Elena Martin.

As he felt the cold water on his face, he anxiously realized that Elena could make a man such as him momentarily forget his goal to become vice president *and* his vow to remain single.

"Aunt Elena, you've got red polka dots on your skin!" Bennie said with wide eyes.

"Polka dots?" she said as she nervously took out a

black evening jacket from her bedroom closet for her first Marriage Connection date. She was so anxious that she'd probably smeared lipstick on her face.

"They're spreading all over!" he went on.

She glanced in the bureau mirror and did a double take. "Oh, no!" she frantically said, seeing red spots on her neck and parts of her face. "Jan, come in here!"

Her sister, who'd stopped by her apartment with the kids to give her moral support for her first date, ran into the bedroom with Tod at her side.

Tod's eyes almost popped out. "Aunt Elena, you've got the chicken pox!"

Jan examined the blotches. "You've got nervous hives," she said, laughing.

"It's not funny!" She grabbed her concealer makeup and applied the flesh-colored cream on her skin.

"Just relax and the spots will disappear," her sister advised as Bennie and Tod ran into the living room to play on her computer.

How could she relax when Garrett had been on her mind all day? "Jan, I can't go on this date."

"You can't back out now," her sister insisted. "Keep reminding yourself that he's perfectly matched for you. *And* he wants to get married, just like you do."

"I'll try. I really will." She didn't want to disappoint her sister, but she knew she'd be thinking about Garrett all evening. *He* was the one she wanted to date.

"El, you better get going," Jan said. "Here's the Marriage Connection card to give to the restaurant maître d'." She handed the engraved card to her. "Call me the second you get home. I don't care if it's three in the morning!"

A few minutes later Elena anxiously parked her car in front of the Tiara Club in Santa Monica Canyon where a valet opened the door for her.

I'm going to meet the man meant for me, she silently

told herself. Why couldn't she believe that? Because of
Garrett, that was why. A black-tuxedoed gentleman
swung open the double doors of the restaurant for her to
enter. Then, she handed the card to the maître d'. He
immediately gave her black jacket to the coat-check lady.

"Follow me, mademoiselle," the maître d' said.

Elena took in the luxurious crystal chandelier and thick
blue carpeting. The candle-lit tables had beige linen ta-
blecloths and napkins butterflied in sterling silver holders
with dazzling silverware at each china place setting.

She hoped she was dressed fancy enough in her jade
velvet spaghetti-strapped dress. She had a string of pearls
around her neck, matching pearl-drop earrings and was
wearing jade pumps.

Her body trembled a little as the maître d' led her to
the door of a private room. She wanted to turn around
and go back home. She didn't want to meet a new man.

"Your date will be here any moment, mademoiselle,"
he said.

As the gentleman opened the door, she glimpsed a for-
mally set table with tall white candles and red roses in a
crystal vase. She could hear soft piano music playing in
the background and noticed a small hardwood dance floor.

"Mademoiselle," he began, "I would like to introduce
your date for the evening."

Elena took a deep breath and turned around to meet the
perfect man matched for her. Her eyes widened when she
saw Garrett standing there!

"Elena Martin meet Garrett Sims," the maître d' said.
"I will have your waiter bring in the champagne." Then
he left and closed the private room door behind him.

"Wow, Elena!" Garrett said, his eyes taking her all in.
"You're my date? I must've hit the jackpot!"

"Garrett, I can't believe—" She was so thrilled that
she could barely speak. "This is so incredible!"

He looked incredible. He was starkly handsome in a

black tuxedo, crisp white shirt and black satin bow tie. The tux jacket stretched across his broad shoulders and solid chest. She felt the urge to throw her arms around his neck and tell him how ecstatic she felt that he was her date!

"You look gorgeous, Eléna," he said in a husky voice, his gaze sensually traveling down her body.

Her skin tingled at his visual caress. "So do you!" she blurted and then blushed, adding, "I mean, you look great, Garrett."

She wanted to ask him a zillion questions about his signing up with the dating service, but she was so flustered being with him that she couldn't remember the name of the service.

After a discreet knock on the door, the waiter entered with two crystal flute glasses of sparkling pink champagne.

Garrett slipped his hand in hers and led her to the dinner table. As he sat across from her, her heartbeat raced when she felt his knees gently touch hers.

"To us," he said, tapping his sparkling glass with hers.

She nodded, unable to believe that her dream had come true. With a trembling hand, she took a sip of the pink bubbly, her eyes never leaving his.

The waiter served an exquisite salad of garden greens with French dressing and then an entreé of baked hen with baby carrots and garlic mashed potatoes.

"Hungry?" Garrett asked, offering her a cut of hen on his fork. "What a stroke of fate that I should be with you tonight," he whispered. "I've got to admit something to you, Elena."

"What?" she asked, feeling like her heart was about to burst with joy at being with him.

"The moment I met you in Stanley's office," he began, "I was majorly attracted to you. I've wanted to be with you ever since."

"You've been on my mind since that meeting, too," she responded, unable to hold back her feelings for him.

He leaned across the small table and gently stroked her cheek, sending chills down her skin. "No wonder the dating service connected us together," he said.

Her heart skipped a beat as his finger slid down her neck, tracing the strand of pearls just above the rise of her breasts.

The waiter came into the room, asking, "Is the dinner pleasing to you?"

"Very pleasing," Garrett replied, his eyes on her, as though he were talking only about being with her.

Elena was so consumed with Garrett that she didn't remember finishing the rest of her meal. Before she knew it, the busboy was clearing the table. Then the waiter carried in a silver tray filled with chocolate éclairs, whipped cream fruit tarts, and creamy cheesecake.

She slipped a slice of sumptuous éclair into Garrett's mouth and then let him lick the whipped cream off the tips of each of her fingers. The desire in his eyes matched her own, and she barely noticed when the maître d' came into the private room.

The soft background piano music switched to a love ballad. The lights dimmed, and kaleidoscope rainbow lights glittered across the shiny dance floor.

Elena felt overwhelmed with nervousness thinking about dancing in Garrett's arms.

"Please dance," the maître d' encouraged. "You will not be disturbed for the last hour of your evening."

Garrett barely noticed the maître d' leave. He couldn't take his eyes off Elena. Her cheeks were slightly flushed. Her ivory breasts swelled over the top of her velvet dress, which hugged the hourglass curves of her body.

He took her hand and led her to the multicolored dance floor. He slipped his arm around her small waist and gently drew her against his body, slowly swaying to the love beat.

"It feels so good to hold you, Elena," he whispered, pressing his palms against the small of her back, guiding her closer to him.

He could smell the vanilla in her hair. He could feel her firm breasts against his chest. He still couldn't believe that he was with her.

Being with Elena, he lost all sense of time, all awareness of where he was. And before he realized it, his mouth was closing over hers, tasting the sweet nectar of her lips. He slid his lips down to her throat.

Wanting to touch every part of her, he slipped his fingers under the spaghetti straps of her dress. He felt her breathing quicken as he lowered the straps and touched her satiny shoulders with his lips. Her skin was so soft, so warm. He reached the hills of her breasts above her dress. He nibbled and kissed her flesh, needing to taste even more of her.

A low moan escaped from her lips as he cupped her velvet-covered breasts in his hands. He could feel her nipples rise against his palms. Her pleasure ignited his body like a lit match.

Garrett forgot that he needed to hold back his feelings and not get deeply involved with Elena. All he was aware of was his powerful need to get closer to her.

Three

Elena was oblivious to the kaleidoscope lights. She could barely hear the love ballad playing. All she could feel were the intense sensations of Garrett's caresses.

She felt so close to him. She felt like he was her dream man come true.

Suddenly the buzzing of a cellular phone startled her back to reality. She realized that the ringing was coming from Garrett's jacket pocket.

She gently released herself from his arms, her skin still burning from his touch.

"I'm sorry," he whispered, pulling the cellular out of his pocket. "I'll take care of it right away."

"It's okay," she whispered back.

As she lifted up the straps of her dress, she noticed him take a few steps off the dance floor to answer the call. Though his voice was low, she couldn't help hearing his words.

"I'm kind of busy, Bert," Garrett said into the phone. "You what?" His voice lowered even more. "Are you sure it might be a new account for me? Who's the owner of the property? I want to talk to him."

Though her cheeks were still warm with arousal, Elena suddenly became aware that Garrett was discussing the possibility of getting a new property management account.

A flood of disappointment washed over her. No matter how close she felt to him during their date, Garrett was still her competitor. He wanted the vice presidency just as much as she did.

Just then she heard Garrett say goodbye and flip closed the cell phone. He turned to her, looking like he had a secret he couldn't tell her. After their intimate moments together on the dance floor, she couldn't help but feel excluded. Yet she knew he had no other choice but to keep silent about his business call.

And she knew she couldn't get emotionally involved with Garrett, not if she wanted Stanley to promote her.

"I really need to get home," she said, grabbing her purse with trembling fingers.

"Elena, I didn't mean to spoil our evening," he began.

"You didn't," she said, avoiding his eyes, wishing she'd never been kissed and caressed by him, because she only wanted more.

"I should never have answered that call," he said.

She wished he hadn't, either. Now there was a barrier between them that she couldn't make go away.

"Garrett, our prearranged dates can't make us forget who we really are," she forced out.

"I don't want it to ruin our evening together."

"I don't, either," she said. "But the fact is that I want that job, too, Garrett. Tonight hasn't changed my goal."

She hated talking business with him, but she had to keep an emotional separation between them. She had to show him that the promotion was as important to her as it was to him.

"Maybe I'm wrong," he began, "but I thought you and I were feeling close to each other tonight."

"We are, we were," she stammered, "but only because of the date. We're business associates, Garrett. I can't have anything more than a platonic relationship with you." Her words felt forced. "I'm obligated by the dating service contract to go on two more dates with you, but we can't date in between."

"What if I don't agree to your rules?" he asked, his eyes locked to hers, as though there was no way they could ever stay apart.

There was a knock at the door, and the maître d' entered. "I hope you enjoyed your evening together."

"Yes, we have," she replied, glancing at Garrett, nervously squeezing her purse in her hand, wishing the evening hadn't ended on a business tone.

"Is there anything else either of you desire?" the man asked.

Garrett's eyes were steady on her. She didn't dare speak. Then he'd know that she desperately desired to be held by him again, wanting their business competition not to matter at all.

"The date was perfect," she finally said.

Then she quickly left the private room, knowing if she stayed a moment longer, she wouldn't have the willpower to stick with her business resolve.

"Elena—" Garrett called out, but before he could follow her, the maître d' handed him a slip of paper.

"Mr. Sims, can I have your signature on this form?" he asked.

Garrett anxiously jotted down his name, confirming that

he and Elena had completed their first prearranged date at the Tiara Club.

As he hurried out of the restaurant, he saw the valet close the door to Elena's car, and she drove off before he could talk to her.

Frustrated, he watched her red taillights disappear on Santa Monica Canyon Road. He wished he'd never answered his friend's call. But Bert, a Realtor who was working late that night at the Trent Realty Company, had just gotten a great tip on a property needing management. A project that could help Garrett get closer to his bid for the vice presidency.

However, at that moment Garrett felt zero interest in the tip. He was more concerned about how that business call had affected Elena.

As he drove down the hilly road of Santa Monica Canyon, he still felt consumed with thoughts of her. In the private room at the Tiara Club, he was so totally captivated by her that he'd completely forgotten she was competing with him at work.

He could still feel the warmth of Elena's swelling breasts above her dress against his lips. He'd yearned to unzip the velvet and put his mouth over her bare nipples.

He could feel his manhood straining against his tuxedo pants just thinking about her. He knew that if Bert hadn't called him with a tip, he would've invited her to his apartment after the Tiara Club.

Why deny it? He wanted to spend the entire Saturday night and all day Sunday holding her in his arms and making love to her.

He pushed his foot down hard on the gas pedal to make the yellow light, knowing he could never pursue a relationship with her. She deserved a man who'd commit his entire life to her. He could never be that man.

Yet, resounding over and over in his head was the

knowledge that the dating service had matched her as the perfect woman for him.

Instead of going to his apartment, he drove toward the After-Hours Pool Hall on Santa Monica Boulevard where he knew Trey would still be shooting some balls.

Trey had been his buddy since he'd moved to Los Angeles. He played on a local baseball team with him. Trey was a cable television technician whose wife had divorced him about the time that Garrett's marriage crumbled.

Garrett remembered the night at the After-Hours Pool Hall when he and Trey vowed to never tie the marital knot again. He knew he could rely on Trey to get his confused thoughts back on solid track.

He walked into the dimly lit pool room, unbuttoning his tux jacket and taking off his bow tie. Guys and gals were drinking beer, listening to the jukebox music and hanging out at pool tables.

He spotted Trey waving him over to a table where he was shooting the bull with a couple of guys.

Trey high-fived him. "How'd the blind date at the Tiara Club go?"

"Not bad," he replied, taking a cue stick and motioning the two ball into the side pocket.

"Sounds like you hit it off with her."

"She's a special lady," he said before he realized it.

"How special?" his friend pursued. "Fun-dates special? Or wedding-march special?"

"Right in between." Feeling tension building in his body, he pointed the five ball toward the corner and tapped it right in.

"You better watch out, Garrett baby. She sounds like the kind of woman who could put the title of husband back on your tax returns."

Hearing himself referred to as a husband made him so disoriented that he slammed the cue ball off the table.

"No chance of that happening," he told his friend.

Just then, a dance beat blared from the jukebox. Trey put down his cue stick and grabbed the hand of red-headed Susie, a legal assistant who often dropped by and played pool with them. Susie and Trey always danced together while Garrett danced with her friend, Cora. But not that night.

He couldn't imagine another woman in his arms, not after holding Elena close to him while dancing at the Tiara Club. He was relieved to see Cora busily chatting with a friend.

He tapped Trey on the shoulder and said over the blasting music, "I'll catch you later!"

"You just got here!" Trey protested as he wiggled his hips to the beat.

"I'm going to crash early."

"I told you," Trey began, smiling mischievously. "She's already infiltrating your brain. Before you know it, she's all you'll be thinking about!"

Garrett forced a grin, shook his head and headed out the front door. But Trey's words pounded at his skull. Because Elena Martin *was* all he was thinking about!

Late that night, while getting ready for bed, Elena's emotions were so chaotic that she almost forgot to call her sister. She quickly dialed the number.

"Jan, you won't believe who my date was," she said. "Garrett Sims, my arch rival for the promotion!"

"Garrett Sims?" her sister asked, surprised. "That's incredible! He's the man you most want to be with."

"Jan, you don't understand. I told Garrett that I can't get personally involved with him."

"What?" her sister asked incredulously over the line. "You found the ideal man for you and you're turning him away?"

"I've got no other choice," she told her. "He's not wasting any time trying to get the vice president job." She explained about his phone call. "I can't let him think that my attraction to him will slow me down."

"How can you possibly keep him out of your mind until the second Marriage Connection date?" Jan asked.

"I don't know," she said, picturing his charcoal eyes looking at her, making her feel so wanted, so desired.

Elena heard Bennie crying in the background.

"El, I've got to go," her sister said. "Bennie's having a monster nightmare."

"Give him a hug and kiss for me," she said and then hung up.

As she slipped under the sheet, she kept telling herself, *I'm going to put Garrett out of my mind. I'm not thinking about him. I'm not!*

But when the alarm woke Elena for work the next morning, her first thought of the day was of Garrett. She realized that she'd been dreaming about him all night.

She hurried out of bed, struggling to keep him romantically out of her consciousness so she could rev up the energy and motivation to charge after property accounts.

At her office she frantically made telephone call after telephone call, checking off the long list of property owners on the Westside whose apartment and commercial buildings she'd seen advertised in the newspaper.

"I'm sorry, Ms. Martin," the hundredth voice told her. "But we've already got a management company."

Frustrated and totally exasperated by her failure to get even one appointment with a building owner, Elena was about to leave her cubicle for a breather when she saw Garrett enter the office. He was walking up to Grace's reception desk.

She quickly sat back down, feeling her pulse race, knowing he was just a few feet away from her.

"Stanley will be with you in a moment, Garrett," she heard Grace say.

Was he meeting with Stanley regarding the account he'd just heard about? If so, she felt like a total failure from her end.

Suddenly, from the edge of her partition, she saw Garrett heading toward her cubicle. She wanted him to know that she was just as successful as he was.

She quickly picked up the phone and started speaking into the dial tone. "Yes, absolutely," she pretended. "Let's meet to discuss your property management needs."

When she glanced up, Garrett was leaning against the smoked glass partition, watching her with appreciative eyes. She felt her hands grow moist with nervousness. She quickly hung up the phone.

"Elena, you forgot to say goodbye to your client," he commented.

She could feel the blood drain out of her face at her fake call. "Sometimes I get so excited about my work," she began, "that I forget the formalities."

He leaned close to her and in a low voice said, "I hope you're still not mad at me about that phone call on our first date."

"Not at all," she whispered, superconscious of his hand resting on her desk, just inches from caressing her body.

"The date was very special to me, Elena," he said.

"Me, too," she admitted.

"Garrett," Grace called out from the reception desk, "Stanley's ready to see you."

"Sure thing, Grace." His warm gaze held hers for a lingering moment, and as he left her cubicle, he said loudly enough for the office to hear, "Thanks, Elena, for those vendor numbers.'' Then he went into Stanley's office.

Grace hurried into her cubicle. ''Elena, I think I've got a property lead for you,'' she said in a hushed voice. She gave her the name of a realty company for an apartment building in Pasadena she heard might need management.

''Grace, you're wonderful!'' Elena said, hugging her.

''Good luck. I want to see a woman vice president running the company!''

With a jolt of energy, Elena phoned the Trenton Realty Company to inquire. She was told that the apartment complex was vacant and needed extensive renovation from the last earthquake. But the agent had no idea if the owner, Mr. Freed, had already chosen a management firm and would check in the office to find out.

As Elena waited on hold, she saw Garrett walk out of Stanley's office. He seemed preoccupied and rushed. He glanced her way, smiled and then quickly left.

Sensing that he was on to something, she didn't waste a moment's time. She hung up and dialed Mr. Freed's number. She kept getting a busy signal. Then her other line rang.

She quickly switched and listened as the upset owner of one of the apartment buildings she managed complained that two of the washers and dryers in the laundry room had stopped working, and tenants were waiting in line.

Elena quickly called her repair vendor and said she'd meet him at the building. She grabbed her bag, thanked Grace again for her help and hurried out of the office to handle the problem.

At the building, while the repairman worked, she called the Pasadena apartment owner again, but Mr. Freed's line was still busy.

Feeling pressured to get her first account, sure that Garrett was ahead of her, she decided to go to Mr. Freed in person.

With excited anticipation, Elena parked her car in front of the ten-story apartment complex in Pasadena. The balconies were filled with leaves and crumbling stucco. Broken windows were boarded up. The walls of the building had snakelike cracks from the last earthquake.

As she entered the uninhabited building, she noticed the owner's name taped onto a mailbox with Penthouse Ten written on it. She went into the elevator and pressed the tenth floor.

The elevator squeaked and shook as it slowly rose to the tenth floor, and she was relieved to get out. She anxiously walked down the hallway and noticed that one door to the penthouse was closed. She turned the corner and up ahead saw an open door.

As she neared it, she heard the voices of two men. Her feet froze in place when she recognized one of the voices as Garrett's.

"Mr. Freed, I think you will be very satisfied with your decision to sign a contract with Grant Property Management," she heard Garrett say to the owner.

"Mr. Sims, I look forward to your handling my building," the man told him.

Elena's body suddenly felt ice-cold. She stepped back from the open door so Garrett wouldn't see her. She leaned against the wall. Her mind was whirling. Garrett had gotten the account she hoped would be hers!

"I'll immediately hire competent vendors to renovate this building to perfect working order," Garrett added. "Of course at a price you will greatly appreciate."

She anxiously bit her bottom lip as she heard the owner laugh. "My accountant will keep me well informed of your budget sheet," the man said. "I hope you will excuse me, Mr. Sims, but I must leave to attend a conference. After you gather all of your files, please close the penthouse door behind you.''

She immediately panicked, wondering if she should dash to the elevator, but she heard the other door of the penthouse around the corner open and close. Then she heard the squeaky elevator descend.

Before she could escape, Garrett stepped into the hallway carrying a stack of folders. He stopped dead in his tracks when he saw her.

''Elena, what're you doing here?''

''The same reason you came,'' she forced out. ''But you beat me to it.''

With a lump in her throat, she turned and headed toward the elevator.

''Elena, wait!'' he called out.

Disappointed and frustrated, she stood near the elevator, frantically pushing the Down button, even though it was already lit.

''You're not being fair,'' he said, suddenly near her.

''*I'm* not being fair?'' she repeated incredulously. ''You're the one that's so gung-ho about getting new accounts that you interrupted our prearranged date to scrounge up an account ahead of me.''

''I didn't mean for that to happen.''

''And on top of that,'' she added in a rush of mixed-up emotion, ''you somehow overheard Grace telling me about *this* building and made sure you got here before me.''

''That's not true,'' he protested.

When the elevator arrived, Elena bolted inside and Garrett followed her into the small space. As the doors closed, she pressed the Lobby button, but the elevator remained on the tenth floor. She kept pressing it and pressing it, but the elevator wouldn't budge.

Garrett set his folders on the floor and moved close to her to get to the control panel. "I'll do it."

"I will," she insisted, trying to act cool and business-like.

He reached across and pressed the Open Door button, then the Close Door button, and the elevator started to squeak and shake as it slowly descended.

Her skin began to perspire under her dress, not from the hot stuffy air, but from Garrett's body so close to hers.

"Elena, I didn't know that you heard about this building, too," he said, his voice low, upset.

"It doesn't matter," she told him, trying to ignore the electrifying heat radiating from his body to hers. "You got to the owner before me, and that's it."

She didn't want to be vulnerable with him, not after he'd just beaten her to her first account, but his sensitivity to her feelings made her weak inside.

"I never meant to hurt you by getting this account," he said. "If I'd known—"

Just then the elevator lights went out, and the elevator suddenly came to a jarring halt, causing her to be pushed into Garrett's arms. She felt his strong hands against her back, steadying her.

"Elena, are you all right?" he asked as he held her close to him in the darkened space.

As long as I'm with you, I'll always be okay, she wanted to say. "I'm fine," she said instead. "What could be wrong with the elevator?"

"When I first arrived in the building, the electricity went off," he told her. "In a few minutes the power will probably come back on."

"Maybe we should press the Emergency button," she said, trying to keep her voice from trembling.

"There's nobody in the building but us."

''Nobody?'' she repeated in almost a whisper.

''Just us,'' he whispered back.

Garrett couldn't resist Elena a moment longer; his body was turning to fire as he held her softness against him in the darkened elevator.

When her eyes held his in a long embrace, his mouth found hers, needing to taste her. She welcomed him by parting her lips. His tongue met hers, mingling and dancing, releasing the passion he'd been holding back.

He glided his hands down the curves of her back, needing to know every intimate inch of her. Then he gently touched her firm derriere over her skirt.

He heard her softly moan against his lips as he pressed her body against his growing manhood. Pleasurable sensations streaked through his frame when she crushed her curves to him.

Needing to feel more of her, he caressed her full breasts over the silken top. Her heartbeat quickened against his palm, and her nipples peaked at his touch.

He slipped his hands under her blouse and fondled her lace-covered globes, desiring even more of her.

He felt her unbutton his jacket. She slid her hands under his shirt, spreading her fingers across his bare chest.

He groaned as she squeezed his nipples between her fingertips. Responding to her passion, he reached for the clasp of her bra, aching to caress her naked breasts.

Just then, the elevator squeaked, shook and then started to slowly move down the shaft. The lights flashed back on. She released her body from his. Her eyes were glassy. Her lipstick a little smeared. Her hair slightly mussed. He wanted to draw her into his arms all over again and never let her go.

The elevator doors opened at the lobby level. He noticed her avoid his eyes as she hurried toward the lobby doors.

"Elena, wait!" he called out.

She stopped and turned to him. "What happened in the elevator was a mistake."

"A mistake?" he repeated, surprised. Then he saw a spark of desire still in her eyes, and he knew she was still feeling the electricity between them, just as he was. "I think you wanted me to kiss you as much I wanted to hold you in my arms."

"We shouldn't have, Garrett," she whispered.

"Why?" he asked.

"I'm interested in only one thing," she told him. "I want that promotion, and I won't let anything stand in my way of getting it, even if it means deliberately keeping a distance from you."

"I see," he said, still aware of the spark radiating between them. "Are you waiting for me to promise never to hold you in my arms again? I can only do that if you promise not to kiss me back."

"You're impossible!" she said, exasperated. "I don't want to see or talk to you unless it's business related!" Then she turned on her heels and quickly left the building.

In her parked car, Elena could barely turn the ignition key. Her skin still felt damp, and her body felt weak from being in Garrett's arms in the elevator.

When she finally got the engine humming, she drove past the rundown apartment building, not daring to look back.

Desperately trying to regain her equilibrium, she remembered that she had to stop at Tony's Pizza Place. She knew her sister was exhausted after working, picking up the kids from the sitter and helping them with homework. So once a week she picked up a large salad and one cheese and pepperoni pizza to bring to Jan's house for dinner.

As she waited for her order to be filled, she couldn't

stop thinking about Garrett. Why did the promotion have no meaning when she was with him?

Suddenly she noticed a young couple hugging and kissing as they waited for their takeout pizza. She could hear the guy whispering to the young woman about how much he loved her. He said he couldn't imagine moving to Nevada without her, but he knew how important her job in L.A. was to her.

She heard the young woman whisper back, "I'll quit my job and find a new one. I don't care what I have to do, as long as we're together."

Suddenly upset, Elena took her container of salad and two boxes of hot pizza and hurried to her car. The young woman's words kept playing through her brain, *I don't care what I have to do, as long as we're together.*

Every time she was with Garrett, she felt exactly the same way. Nothing mattered to her except being close to him. Did he feel the same way about her? Would he ever want a future with her?

She immediately halted her thoughts. She couldn't think that way about Garrett, not when she needed the vice president salary raise for her family. She had to keep to her word and not call or see him unless it was related to business.

Her mind was in turmoil as she entered Jan's house. She came to an abrupt halt when she saw her sister sitting at the kitchen table with dark circles under her eyes.

"Jan, what's the matter?" she asked, setting the food on the counter.

"The elderly woman I care for every Saturday morning is going to be put into a convalescent home in one week," she replied. "This Saturday is my last day with her. I've got the agency looking for other work for me, but I can't afford losing even one Saturday paycheck."

"Don't worry, I'll be paying the mortgage for this

month," Elena told her, feeling the pressure of money striking her again. "You'll find another senior citizen to care for on Saturdays by the time the next round of bills arrives."

She didn't dare tell her sister that her savings were dwindling. She had to go full-force after the promotion.

"El, it's not just my job," Jan went on. "Tod's upset because all of his baseball teammates have a father or uncle to play with them at the all-male family game this Saturday. But he has no man in his life to go with him."

"Oh, no," Elena said, knowing how important baseball was to her nephew. "What about your neighbor, what's-his-name, down the street? The one who repairs your car."

Just then, Tod walked into the kitchen with Bennie. "Aunt Elena, the guy doesn't even know how to throw a ball," Tod said. "I need someone who can pitch, because I'm a good catcher." He turned to his mother. "Did you ask her, Mom?"

"Ask me what?" Elena questioned.

Tod looked at her with hopeful eyes. "Can your boy-friend, Garrett, play this Saturday on the team with me?"

Her boyfriend. She wished! She nervously opened the pizza boxes and began dishing out slices on paper plates to her nephews. "I can't ask Garrett," she pushed out.

"Why not?" Jan pursued.

As her nephews gobbled the pizza, Elena leaned closer to her sister and whispered, "I told Garrett that I'm not calling him unless it's related to work. He'll think I'm encouraging him into a relationship with me."

"Aren't you?"

"Yes—I mean, no!" she said. "Not until I've got the vice presidency."

"Please, Aunt Elena," Tod begged. "Garrett said that

he pitches on a team in Santa Monica. It'll be so cool having him play in the game with me on Saturday.''

The hope in her nephew's eyes made it impossible for her to disappoint him. ''Okay, okay, I'll ask him. But I can't promise he'll say yes.''

Tod grabbed the phone. ''Let's find out!''

''Now?'' She needed time to figure out how to ask Garrett in a way that wouldn't make him think she was looking for an excuse to be with him, even if she really was! ''Tod, I need to wait until I get back to my apartment. I don't have his home number.''

Jan pulled out the telephone book. ''I'll find it. Here it is.''

Tod was already dialing it. ''It's ringing, Aunt Elena!''

Her stomach was in knots as he handed her the phone. When she heard Garrett answer, her mind went blank, panicking about what to say to him.

Four

"Hi, Garrett," Elena began, trying not to sound too nervous.

"Elena?" he asked, surprised.

"Did I catch you at a bad time?"

"Not at all," he said, his voice rising with anticipation. "I never expected you to call me at home."

She could hear the warmth and excitement in his voice at her contacting him. Her body temperature immediately rose.

"Actually, I'm calling as a favor to my nephew, Tod," she said, struggling to keep a cool voice. She explained about Tod's needing a male baseball player to play with his team at the game on Saturday morning. "I was wondering, if you're not busy, could you—"

"Tell Tod to put on his catcher's mitt a few minutes before the game so we can warm up."

"You'll do it?"

"I feel honored that you asked me."

"Garrett, you're wonderful!" she blurted without thinking, noticing Tod beaming from ear to ear. She quickly gave him the address of the Little League field. "Thanks so much for helping us out."

"Anytime." His deep masculine voice filtered through her body like smooth honey.

When he hung up, she cleared her throat, praying that her sister and nephews didn't see the powerful effect just talking with him had on her. "Jan, you need to drop off Tod early so Garrett can practice with him."

"Can you go, El?" her sister asked. "I'm working Saturday morning, remember? I'll drop off Bennie at his friend's house. Can you stay for Tod's game?"

Her entire being wanted to go, but she knew she couldn't be with Garrett on a personal basis, not when she needed to see him as her business competitor.

"You're putting me in an awkward spot, Jan."

"Please, Aunt Elena," Tod asked. "We'll have a great time with Garrett."

That was what she was afraid of! "Okay," she finally said, anxiously taking a bite of pizza, telling herself that she'd focus her entire attention on her nephew at the game and not Garrett.

But her palpitating heart told her differently!

Saturday morning, as Elena drove Tod to the Little League field, she was as nervous as if she was going on a date with Garrett.

I'm going to the game to be with my nephew, she silently told herself. *To be with Tod.*

The moment she parked her car, she spotted Garrett sitting on the back of his Mustang wearing a pitcher's glove and flipping a baseball up and down in his hand.

He was wearing white baseball pants and a red jersey with matching baseball cap.

He immediately stood up and smiled when he saw her. Her heartbeat quickened. He's a business associate, that's it, she told herself over and over. But her hands were perspiring, and her skin began to sizzle, even though the morning air was still cool and she was wearing shorts and a tank top.

"Garrett, are you ready to warm up?" Tod called out as he hopped out of Elena's car, running toward him with his catcher's mitt.

"Sure thing, Tod!" Garrett said, but his eyes were on Elena as she locked her car door and started walking toward them.

Her streaked-blond hair glittered under the Southern California sun. His gaze took in the way her white shorts hugged her hips, accentuating her sleek long legs, and the way her round breasts filled out her orange tank top.

He wanted to take her into his arms right that very moment. She's a family woman, he firmly reminded himself. She needs a husband at her side.

As he practice pitched with Tod, he wondered if he'd made a mistake saying yes to playing on Tod's team. He didn't want to send the wrong message to Elena that he was looking to be part of her family.

Yet, as he threw the ball to Tod, he found himself wondering what it would be like to have a son like Tod—with a wife like Elena.

"Garrett, look out for the ball!" Tod called out after he threw it.

Garrett quickly caught the flying ball in his glove, feeling a rush of anxiety over his marriage thoughts.

"Garrett, I really appreciate your coming for Tod," Elena said from behind him.

He turned to her, completely mesmerized by her presence. "I hope you're planning to stay for the game," he said.

"Definitely," she replied, heading toward the bleachers. "I want to see if you're as good on the ball field as you are getting new management accounts."

Though she had a teasing tone, he sensed that deep down she was still hurting from his getting that last property account before her. As he pitched the ball to Tod, he regretted ever agreeing to compete with her for accounts.

Just then, Tod waved him to the dugout with his team. As Garrett sat on the bench with the players, Tod plopped down next to him.

"Do you think we're gonna win, Garrett?" the boy excitedly asked.

"With you and me in there," he said. "We can't lose."

"I'm sure glad you came," Tod went on. "So is my aunt."

"Really?" he asked, surprised.

"Yeah, this morning, I heard her tell my mom that you're the perfect man for her, but then she said something about a job being in the way."

"Play ball!" the umpire yelled out.

Garrett high-fived Tod as the team took the field. Then he stood on the pitcher's mound. For an instant his eyes met Elena's in the bleachers. She quickly glanced away, as though she'd been staring at him for a while but didn't want him to know.

The perfect man for her, he thought. He was sure Tod had overheard Elena discussing the dating service and her being matched to him.

What if she really did think of him as the right man for her?

He hurled the ball to Tod to warm up as the batter headed for the plate. He knew he could never be the ideal man for any woman, especially to someone as special as Elena.

The umpire called time, so the batter could loosen up his swing. Garrett glanced at his watch. He'd promised Trey that he'd help paint his apartment right after the game. He knew he couldn't stay after the game with Elena. He might end up saying things to her that he knew he could never live up to.

A while later, as the game neared the end, with Tod's team just one run ahead, Garrett waited in the dugout as the other team's last hard-hitting player got up to bat. He noticed that Elena had left the bleachers and was standing a few feet behind the fence near home plate. She was right in the line of fire when the batter hit a foul. The ball flew high up over the fence, bounced off the roof of the snack bar and hit Elena in the chest.

Garrett felt his breath knocked out of him. He ran out of the dugout toward her. Garrett rushed Elena away from the crowd into the back seat of his car, needing to take care of her.

"Let me take a look," he said.

Without thinking, he pulled up her orange tank top and gently touched her ribs below her bra. "Does it hurt here?"

She shook her head, her eyes on him, trusting, depending on him. He noticed a slightly reddened area just above the white lace. He gently touched the bruise.

"Ouch," she uttered.

"Sorry."

He suddenly became conscious of his fingers on the swell of her breast, and her dark nipples protruding against the lace. He felt his body respond, and he gently pulled down her top.

"You might have a fracture," he forced out. "We better get X rays taken, just in case."

A few minutes later, he had Tod in the car, and he drove Elena to City Hospital Emergency Room. With one hand around Tod's shoulder and the other holding hers, he entered the emergency room and headed toward the registration desk.

"Garrett, I don't have my insurance card with me," Elena said in a concerned voice.

"Don't worry, we're on the same company plan," he reassured her. "I'll handle it."

He couldn't believe how easy the words came out. He was taking care of her as though she was his—

"Ma'am, can I have your medical card please," the intake clerk asked Elena.

"Here's mine," Garrett told her, handing over his card. "If you call the eight-hundred number on the back, you can confirm Elena Martin's eligibility with the plan."

"What is your relationship to the patient?" the woman asked as she input the information into her computer.

The words flew out. "I'm her boyfriend," he replied.

From the way Elena warmly squeezed his hand, he knew he'd made a big mistake with that answer. Why had he said it? Because at that moment, he felt like she *was* his girlfriend. Yet, he knew he was just dreaming. She'd never stay for long with him. He wasn't that lucky in a relationship.

"Elena Martin!" a nurse called out in the waiting room.

He wanted to go in with her, but he knew he couldn't. "I'll wait here and keep Tod busy," he told her.

"Thanks, Garrett," she said, her gaze holding his for a long moment, and then she followed the nurse into the examining room.

Garrett couldn't sit still. He kept glancing at his watch, worried about Elena, wondering why she was in there so long. He noticed Tod standing near the food machines and gave him some money for chips and soda.

What seemed like eons later, Garrett was relieved to see Elena return to the waiting room with some color back in her cheeks.

"No fractures," she told him. "Just a bruise that should heal pretty quickly."

"Terrific!" He went to hug her but stopped, knowing her bruise might hurt.

She stood on her toes and kissed him on the cheek. "You're a great guy."

Her complimentary words took him by surprise. Before he could respond, he felt Tod pulling at his shirt.

"Here's your change, Garrett," the boy said. "Thanks for the snack."

Elena stared at Garrett. "How much do I owe you?"

"Plenty," he said kiddingly, knowing he owed *her* for letting him briefly share in her life.

When he returned Elena and Tod to her car at the Little League field, he felt a pull to be with her longer.

"Are you sure you can drive home okay?" he asked. "I could give you a lift and later you could get your car."

"We're not far from Jan's house," she said and then added, "Why don't you stop by? Jan should be home from work by now. I could make you lunch."

His impulse was to say yes, but a red flag went up in his brain. She wanted to introduce him to her sister. She was drawing him closer to her family, which meant only one thing. She was thinking about a serious relationship with him—a relationship he knew he'd never be able to fulfill.

He anxiously glanced at his watch, realizing he'd completely forgotten about his painting commitment to Trey. "Elena, thanks, but I can't," he told her. "I was supposed to be at my friend's house an hour ago."

"Oh, sure," she quickly replied, her voice dropping. "I've kept you long enough already."

Before he got a chance to explain, she hurried out of his car, and in the next moment, she drove off with Tod.

As he headed for Trey's apartment, he realized that he'd hurt her feelings. He hadn't meant to act cool to her, when he felt just the opposite. He wanted to go to her sister's. He wanted to get more involved in her life. But deep inside, he didn't trust that a relationship could ever last for him.

Frustrated with himself, he parked in front of Trey's apartment building and slammed out of his car.

Elena entered her sister's kitchen with Tod, upset with herself for asking Garrett to lunch. What reason would he have to come? Wasn't she the one who demanded that they keep their relationship on a business level?

"Tod, who won the game?" her sister asked as she prepared sandwiches.

"We were leading," her nephew excitedly replied. "You should've seen Garrett pitch, but we had to leave early to go to the emergency room."

"Emergency room?" Jan repeated worriedly. "Where did you get hurt?"

"Not me, Mom," he said. "Aunt Elena."

"I got hit in the chest by a foul ball," Elena explained. "I'm fine now."

"You should've seen Garrett take care of her, Mom," Tod added. "He even told the hospital lady that he was her boyfriend!" Then he raced after his little brother into the other room.

Jan stared at her with a knowing expression. "He's getting *very* serious about you."

"He didn't really mean it about the boyfriend thing," Elena told her, hurriedly explaining about not having her medical insurance card. "He had to tell the hospital clerk that he was more than a co-worker to me because—"

"Because why?" her sister questioned.

Her heart was hammering. "I don't know, Jan," she said, feeling confused. "When I asked him over to meet you, he immediately pulled away."

"Of course he did," her sister went on. "You keep putting the promotion as a barrier between you."

"I have to," she said. "I can't look for another job because I've worked hard to be considered for this promotion, and if Stanley ever found out about Garrett and me—"

"Was Stanley in the laundry room with you and Garrett?" Jan cut in. "Did he see you and Garrett kissing on your Marriage Connection date?"

"No, but—"

"Your boss doesn't have to know about your personal life with Garrett," she rushed on. "If you keep your relationship with him outside the office, how will he find out?"

"Sometimes I'm not sure if Garrett really wants a relationship with me," she said.

"Of course he does," Jan continued. "You're just afraid that he might not make a commitment to you. Get rid of that fear for good, El. He signed the Marriage Connection agreement, remember?"

"Yes, but—"

"Face up," her sister added. "You've finally met a terrific guy who cares about you *and* is looking for a wife."

Her stomach filled with butterflies. "Jan, I hope you're right."

Early that evening Garrett forcefully rolled ivory-colored paint onto the living room wall of Trey's apartment. Loud rock music boomed from the radio, but he barely heard a guitar chord. He was scarcely aware of paint speckles splashing on to his arms and face.

He kept hearing Elena's voice inviting him to her sister's and his refusing. Had he hurt her feelings really badly? Should he call her?

Blinded with confusion, he vigorously stroked up and down the wall.

"Garrett, hold up!" Trey called out. "You're painting over the frame of my aluminum window!"

He suddenly focused on his sloppy work. "Geez, I'm sorry," he apologized, quickly grabbing a rag and wiping the wet paint off the window frame.

"What's with you today?" his friend asked. "Are you still having pangs about turning down Elena's lunch invitation?"

"I'm not feeling any pangs," he said, trying to convince himself.

"Good, because I got us a double date for tonight," Trey went on. "I met a great lady on a cable job whose close friend is in town for the weekend. We can go out to dinner and then catch a movie."

"I can't," he replied, quickening his painting strokes on the wall.

"Why not?" his friend pursued. "You said you had no plans, and we've gone on double dates before."

"I'm not in the mood." Feeling completely unsettled, he put down the paint roller and grabbed his car keys. "I need to run an errand. I'll be right back."

Under the evening streetlights, Garrett got into his Mustang, picked up the cell phone and dialed Elena's number. He didn't want to use Trey's phone. He couldn't handle his buddy asking more questions about his feelings for her when he didn't have answers even for himself.

His heart dropped with disappointment when he heard

Elena's voice echo on the answering machine, "I'm not home right now. Please leave a message after the tone, and I'll get back to you."

The machine beeped, and the words flew out of his mouth, as though they were pent up for a millennium. "I wish I was with you, Elena," he said into the answering machine. "I've been thinking about you." He rolled his eyes for being so blunt. "I'm just hoping you feel better."

He hung up, still feeling unfinished. Before returning to Trey's, he drove to a minimall, hoping to somehow make up for rejecting her invitation.

"El, why don't you sleep over?" Jan asked after tucking the boys in bed that night.

Elena opened the front door. "Thanks, but not tonight," she said, needing to be alone with her thoughts about Garrett.

"Don't hold back with him, El," her sister said, reading her mind. "I think you may have found *The One*."

Elena hugged her sister and then drove home. As she walked toward her apartment door, she noticed a glass vase at her doorstep with a sparkling spray of rainbow carnations.

She sucked in her breath as she read the card. Thinking about you. Garrett.

She practically floated into her apartment with the vase of flowers and then saw the answering machine flashing. She couldn't believe it when she heard his voice saying that he wished he was with her.

Oh, Garrett, I want to be with you, too! she thought.

She felt the urge to call him, but she was too nervous about the idea. She didn't want to push him, like she'd done by inviting him to her sister's.

She undressed and put on a silk nightgown. She laid down on her bed, trying to make a list of property owner phone numbers she planned to call at work. But she couldn't stop thinking about Garrett.

She glanced at the clock radio. It was only ten o'clock. She was dying to talk to him. Just as she was about to pick up the phone, it rang against her fingertips. Her pulse raced when she heard Garrett's voice on the line.

"Elena, did I wake you?" he asked.

"Oh, no, I was just lounging in bed," she replied.

"Me, too," he said.

She was suddenly aware of being in her nightgown with him so close on the other end of the line.

"I love the flowers," she said, trying to keep her voice steady.

"How's your bruise?" he asked. "Is it still very red?"

"I don't know," she replied. "I'll look." She unbuttoned the top of her nightgown. "It's a little black-and-blue, and it feels a bit tender."

He was silent a moment. "I wish I was lying in bed with you," he whispered.

A hot sensation sizzled through her limbs. "I wish you were here, too," she whispered back, wanting to immediately invite him over.

Suddenly the list of property owners slipped off the bed and fell to the floor, reminding her of the job she needed to get over him.

"Garrett, I think I better get to sleep," she forced out.

"You're right, it's late," he said. "Good night, Elena."

When she hung up, her skin felt moist under her nightgown. Her body yearned to be held by him. She wanted to believe that her sister was right. But he was already ahead of her in getting new accounts. She had to surpass him to get the salary increase she desperately needed for her family.

She picked up the list, trying to center her energy on a plan to get at least two accounts this week to equal his.

Yet her mind kept drifting back to one thing. Her second Marriage Connection date with Garrett. She hadn't received a notice yet of where the date would take place. All she knew was that she couldn't wait to be alone with him again.

She laid back on the bed, dreaming about lying in his arms and feeling his lips on hers. The list slipped from her fingers as she fantasized about making love to him.

Monday morning, as Garrett arrived at an old apartment building he managed in Culver City, he knew that if Elena had said the word over the phone, he would've hopped out of bed, gotten dressed and raced over to her apartment. But she didn't.

Why should she? She had no reason to get intimately involved with him when he'd made no future promises to her.

As Garrett walked to the apartment of a tenant who was behind in rent, he tried to think of Elena as a woman passing through his life, just like his ex-wife ended up being. But he couldn't. He felt Elena deep in his heart in a way that he never had with his ex-wife.

He knocked on the tenant's door, not looking forward to the task at hand.

An unshaven man in his late thirties opened the door. Two little boys were at his side, staring up at Garrett. The little boys reminded him of Elena's nephews.

"Mr. Carlisle, I need the check for your three-months' back rent," Garrett began, dreading his next words. "Otherwise, the owner wants you evicted."

"Mr. Sims," the tenant nervously replied, "I was laid off my job. My wife has medical problems. Last week I went on a job interview, and I think I got it. But I won't know for a few days. Can you wait a little longer?"

Garrett shifted uncomfortably on his feet. He knew the owner's answer to that question would be a flat no.

"You've got two weeks," he told him instead, knowing the owner was going to bury him for it.

"Thanks, Mr. Sims, thanks so much," the man said, looking relieved, protectively holding the hands of his children.

In his car, Garrett called the owner on his cell phone to let him know. He had to hold the phone a few inches from his ear as the owner yelled that he hadn't carried out his orders and even threatened to terminate his building contract with Grant Property Management.

"Don't worry, the tenant will pay," Garrett insisted. "Why would I have given the man an extra two weeks if I wasn't positive?"

However, when Garrett clicked off the phone, he knew he was hanging off the edge with that one. Why had he taken a chance with that tenant? Elena's sister's struggle to care for her two sons flashed in his mind. He realized that being a part of Elena's family had already made a major impact on his life.

His thoughts were interrupted by the sound of his cell phone ringing.

"Garrett, can you meet me for a quick lunch meeting?" Stanley asked over the line. "Elena will be there. I want to check out where the two of you stand in the new account area for the promotion."

"Sure, where?" he replied, feeling uneasy, hoping that Elena had come up with new accounts to match his.

"The Sea Gate Café on the Santa Monica Promenade," he replied. "See you in a little while."

A few minutes later Garrett entered the café and immediately spotted Elena sitting at a table toward the back with Stanley. She looked radiant in a wine-colored blouse. The moment he approached their table, he could see the distress in her eyes and wondered whether she'd gotten any accounts yet. How was he going to tell Stanley that not only had he gotten two accounts, but he had another one pending, when he didn't know where she stood with hers?

"Stanley, how are you?" he said, shaking his outstretched hand.

Then he took Elena's hand in his, yearning to put her palm to his lips. But with Stanley around, he had to be on his best businesslike behavior. "Nice to see you, Elena."

"I need to make this a short lunch. Elena and I have already ordered." Stanley glanced at his watch. "What's the new account status?"

"Well—" Elena began with a worried look in her eye.

Before she could finish, Garrett cut in, "It's tough out there, Stanley. So far I've only lucked out on one property with the help of a Realtor friend of mine."

Elena caught his eye. She knew he was deliberately neglecting to tell Stanley about his second account.

"I know the market is tight," his boss responded. "What about you, Elena?"

"I've got something pending," she hedged.

"Where's the location of the property?" Stanley pursued.

"Location?" She nervously bit her bottom lip. "Oh, it's—"

"Here's your roast beef sandwich, Stan!" Garrett interrupted as the waitress appeared with their orders.

"Umm, I'm starving," his boss said, taking a big bite.

For the next few minutes Garrett kept Stanley busy discussing their tasty lunches. He noticed Elena picking at her sesame chicken salad. He wished he could lift her spirits, but how could he when he was the one making her feel low with his two accounts?

When Stanley finished his lunch, he glanced at his watch. "Sorry for the short meeting, but I've got another appointment." He arose from the table. "Elena, I'll catch you back at the office to talk further about that new account you're working on."

"Of course," she said. "I'll tell you all the details."

The moment Stanley left the restaurant, she turned to him. "Why did you hide your second account from Stanley?" she demanded.

"I didn't want to tell him that I already had two when I wasn't sure what you had."

"I can take care of myself, Garrett." As she grabbed her bag from the table, she accidentally knocked it to the floor, spilling out her lipstick, keys, tissues and other paraphernalia.

He squatted with her to the floor to help gather up her stuff.

"Elena, I'm sorry if I insulted you."

"It doesn't matter," she said, her voice cracking. "I haven't even gotten one account yet."

He saw her eyes get misty, and he touched her hand. "Do you have a few minutes?" he asked. "We could go for a ride in my car."

"I need to get back to the office."

"Just for a little while."

She hesitated. "Okay."

Outside, as he opened the door to his car for her, he noticed her setting the alarm on her wristwatch. He knew she was worried about being late for her talk with Stanley. Why was he inviting her to go for a ride when they both needed to get back to work?

Five

On the hill of Pebble Park, overlooking the Pacific Ocean, Elena couldn't believe she'd agreed to go with Garrett for a ride. She watched him get out a blanket from the trunk of his car to spread on the grass.

She tried to put all work-related worries out of her mind. All she wanted to think about was lying on the blanket in the comfort of his arms.

She sat on the blanket and hugged her bent knees as she gazed out at the blue Pacific. She noticed a couple of bees in the area and hoped the ocean breeze would steer them in another direction.

"I come here to think sometimes," Garrett told her as he lay down next to her, plucking a blade of grass and putting it between his lips.

With his warm eyes on her and with the way he toyed with the grass in his mouth, she couldn't help but think about his lips trailing across her naked body.

"It really is quiet here," she said, trying to shift her attention away from her sensual response to him.

"Tell me, Elena," he began as he gently glided the blade of grass up her bare leg. "What do you want more than anything right now?"

You, you, you! she wanted to say. Instead, she tried to act cool and businesslike to keep the emotional distance she needed to compete with him for the job.

"I want only one thing," she said. "To become vice president of the company."

"A career goal, nothing more?" he asked, surprised.

"That's it," she replied.

"I don't believe you," he said with a teasing glint in his eyes.

"Why not?" she asked, her skin tingling as he slid the grass above her knee to her thigh.

"I think you want a lot more than that job."

Her defenses melted as his eyes held hers in a warm embrace. "I wish I weren't competing with you, Garrett," she whispered. "I wish—"

He drew her into his arms, and his mouth covered hers. She mingled her tongue with his, needing to feel close to him. As she slid down next to him on the blanket, he gently pressed the length of his body to hers.

She felt his hard chest against her breasts and his rock-hard thighs against her legs. She felt like she was lying in bed with him. His hands glided up and down her back, and she pressed her entire body to his.

As she slid her palms up the bulging muscles of his arms, she heard a buzzing sound near her ear.

She slowly opened her eyes and saw a swarm of bees flying above them.

"Garrett!" she shrieked. "Bees! All over!"

He held her still. "We're okay," he said. "Get up very slowly."

"I hate bees!" she choked out, carefully standing up.

He gently picked up the blanket and protectively wrapped the wool around her. "Let's go!" he said, getting her to his car, which was parked in the secluded lot.

He'd no sooner gotten them safely settled inside than she heard buzzing near her ear again. "Is there a bee in the car?" she squealed.

"Don't move," he warned. "It's in your hair."

"Get it out!"

As he pressed the button on his door to open her window, he leaned close to her and swatted the bee from her hair out the window, quickly closing the window again.

"Are you okay?" he asked, his body still leaning against hers.

"I think so." Her heartbeat sped up as she smelled the musk scent of his manly body close to hers.

When his mouth touched her neck, a streak of heat rushed through her veins. She felt the pleasure of his lips gliding down her throat, trailing kisses over her skin, igniting her entire body.

She felt his fingers land on the buttons of her blouse. He hesitated and whispered, "Do you want me to stop, Elena?"

Her brain signaled to tell him that she needed to get back to the office. But as his fingertip grazed a nipple over her blouse, her rational mind stopped working. And her heart and body took control. She passionately pressed her lips to his with her answer.

Garrett was no longer aware of being at Pebble Park. He was totally engulfed in Elena. As he tasted the honey flavor of her lips, he undid the buttons of her blouse. He pushed her blouse aside and gazed at her bountiful lace-covered breasts, heaving with each short breath she took.

As he slipped the fabric down her shoulders, he glided his thumb along the top edge of her bra down to the soft valley of her warm breasts. Her nipples hardened in response, and his mouth grazed the lace covering her flesh.

A moan escaped from her lips, and her excited response sent a jolt of fire through him. He could feel her heartbeat wildly pounding against his mouth.

His blood pulsated through his veins as he reached for the front clasp of her bra, needing to feel the nakedness of her. Just as he was about to unclasp the latch, the alarm on her wristwatch went off.

"I—I've got to get back to the office," she stammered.

He was so enveloped in his feelings for her that he forgot he was on his lunch hour. He forgot that he had to get back to work. All that existed was Elena.

He turned on the ignition as she slipped on her blouse. "Elena, I'm sorry I made you late. I lost all sense of time."

"Don't apologize," she said, her eyes sparkling with a warmth that turned his insides to jelly. "I forgot the time, too."

As he drove, his body tensed in the seat, realizing that he'd allowed himself to get too close to her, when he knew he shouldn't. But how could he stop himself? Whenever he was near her, he wanted her even more than the last time he was with her.

When he dropped her off at the Santa Monica Promenade to get her car, he could see the worry return to her eyes as she hurried off. He knew she was nervous about talking to Stanley. He wanted to reassure her that everything would be okay, but how could he, when he was the one causing her to feel pressured at work?

He gunned up his car and headed for the freeway toward the realty office where his friend, Bert, worked. He was so tense that his hand muscles cramped from holding the steering wheel too tight.

* * *

As Elena entered the office, her skin still burned from Garrett's touch. She prayed that the junior property managers and Grace couldn't somehow tell that she'd just been in Garrett's arms.

She said a quick hello to Grace and hurried to her desk behind the partition. In a frenzy she tried to come up with a story to tell Stanley about her nonexistent new account. But her mind was preoccupied with how close she felt to Garrett.

If her wristwatch alarm hadn't gone off, how far would she have gone with him? Very far, her inner voice answered. Because during their intimate moments in his car, her relationship with him had reached a deeper level. She could feel it when he touched her, when he kissed her. She knew neither of them could talk about it, not when the promotion was glaring them in the face.

"Elena," Grace said, peeking into her cubicle. "Stanley just called. He's not feeling well and won't be back to the office this afternoon. He said he'll talk to you tomorrow."

Breathing a sigh of relief, she grabbed the telephone, thankful that she had extra time to drum up a new account before he questioned her. She tried to concentrate on topping Garrett.

She randomly called real estate offices on the Westside, asking if the agents had recently sold an apartment or commercial building. After repeatedly hearing no, she nearly jumped out of her chair when one female agent said, "As a matter of fact, I just purchased two luxury buildings in Westwood for a client of mine."

Two buildings! she silently screamed with excitement.

"Has he gotten a management firm to handle the two properties?" Elena hopefully asked.

"I don't think so," the woman replied. "But I haven't talked to him in a few days, so I'm not sure."

After getting the owner's name, phone number and the addresses of the luxury buildings, Elena practically flew out of the office, quickly telling Grace she'd be right back. Within a few minutes, she drove to the apartment buildings, which were side by side on Wilshire Boulevard in upscale Westwood.

This time, she was determined to be very prepared before she called the owner for an appointment. If she got the account for those buildings, she'd be equal with Garrett.

She struggled to ignore the emotional bond she felt toward him, so she could concentrate on the Westwood buildings. She walked around the exterior of the two luxury apartment buildings with pad and pencil in hand to familiarize herself with the properties.

But Garrett kept popping into her head. She didn't want to pursue ways to equal him at a business venture. She just wanted to love him.

She entered the crystal-chandeliered lobbies of the two complexes and checked out the number of apartments in each. She glanced at the almost-expired elevator service contracts and jotted down the expiration dates on a pad.

After noting every detail of each building, she left.

Back at the office she quickly placed a call to the owner, Mr. Slater, and spoke with his secretary, telling her that she'd visited the buildings and wanted to make an appointment to meet him. Since Mr. Slater was booked solid in the morning, the secretary gave her a two-o'clock afternoon appointment.

Elena hung up the phone, filled with fiery energy. She had to keep her hand off the phone to stop from calling Garrett. She knew it was crazy, but she wanted to share her excitement about the appointment.

Instead she grabbed a stack of papers and went into the file room. She knew she couldn't tell a soul about the appointment with Mr. Slater, even Garrett. She couldn't take any chances that he might get to the account before her.

At the Trent Realty office, Garrett stood beside Bert, glancing through the just-sold listings of every residential and commercial building on the market throughout Southern California on the computer screen. He wished he could shake off his feeling of guilt at looking for another account, knowing Elena still hadn't gotten her first.

"Garrett, you owe me breakfast, lunch and dinner for this," Bert kidded as he scrolled down the listings.

"How about box seats for a Dodgers game?" he asked, pulling out four tickets he'd bought for Bert, his wife and two kids.

Bert grinned. "I'll get you *two* new accounts for this!"

As his friend continued scanning, Garrett knew that if he was competing with anyone else, he wouldn't question his aggressive pursuit. But not with Elena.

"Here we go," his friend said. "Two luxury apartment buildings just purchased in Westwood."

"Who's the new owner?"

"Let me see," Bert replied, checking further. "Will you look at that."

"What?" he asked, staring at the screen.

"You just lucked out, Garrett," his friend said. "I know the owner. I sold Ralph Slater three buildings in Huntington Beach a few years ago."

"Can I use your name when I call him?" he asked.

"I'll give him a buzz right now," Bert said, picking up the phone. "I haven't talked to Slater since he beat me at golf."

As Bert talked on the phone, Garrett anxiously stared out the window at the tall, spindly palm trees swaying in the dry Santa Ana wind, thinking about Elena. Something deep inside told him to wait on this account.

Before he could stop Bert, his friend hung up the phone. "Garrett, it's all set," Bert said. "Slater is stacked from morning to afternoon with appointments tomorrow. I told him that you're the best in the business, but I forgot to tell him the name of your company. As a favor he immediately made room in his schedule for nine in the morning."

There was no backing out now. "I owe you another set of Dodgers tickets," Garrett said, firmly shaking Bert's hand.

Garrett left the realty office, but before going to Aunt Rosie's for a visit, he drove to Elena's apartment. He got out of his car, needing to see her, feeling so guilty that he couldn't stand it a moment longer. However, as he walked toward her apartment door, he realized that he had no idea what he was going to say.

In her apartment Elena turned on the shower water, about to step in. Her sister would be dropping by in a few minutes while the kids were in karate class. She couldn't wait to tell her about the appointment she got with the owner of the two luxury apartment buildings.

She heard the doorbell ring. Thinking her sister had arrived a few minutes early, she turned off the water, threw on a cotton minirobe over her nakedness and pulled open the door.

"Jan, you got here so—" She stopped when she saw Garrett standing there. Her voice instinctively softened. "I thought you were my sister."

"You're busy," he said as his gaze traveled down the length of her shortie robe.

She was instantly aware of being naked under the fabric, and she could feel her nipples harden against the cotton.

"Come in," she said, trying to hold back the excitement that he'd come to see her.

As he entered, his manly presence immediately filled the living room. She wanted to offer him everything in her place. She wanted him to feel completely at home. She wanted him to stay indefinitely.

"Elena, the account thing between us really bothers me," Garrett began, standing so near her that she wanted to sink into his arms.

"I bet you're getting nervous about the new properties I might be getting now," she said in a teasing way.

His eyes widened. "What new properties?"

"I've got an incredible one that I can't tell you about."

"Great, I mean, you have?" he asked, hopefully.

She smiled. "I'm going to top you, Garrett Sims."

"Are you now?" he asked, gently pushing strands of hair away from her eyes.

"You don't stand a chance with me," she told him, her voice quivering a little as his thumb outlined her lips.

"No chance at all, huh?" he murmured as he pressed his warm lips to her forehead.

She couldn't remember answering. She was suddenly in his arms with her mouth meeting his. Without thinking, she stood on her tiptoes and tightened her arms around his neck, pressing her body against his. His hands moved up and down the back of her minirobe.

She held her breath as she felt him pull up the hem and grasp her bare buttocks in both hands.

"Garrett," she whispered, softly moaning as he squeezed her naked bottom.

The ringing of the telephone broke through her consciousness. She released her aroused body from his and answered it.

"El, I'm running a few minutes late," her sister said over the line. "I'll be at your place in ten minutes."

Her body was throbbing with desire as she glanced over at Garrett, who was glancing at her books on the shelf, giving her privacy.

"El, are you still there?" Jan asked.

"Yes," she half replied.

"Who's in the room with you?"

She lowered her voice to a whisper. "Garrett."

"Oh, wow!" Jan said, her voice rising with excitement. "I don't have to come at all if you'd prefer to—"

"I'll see you in a little while, Jan," she quickly said and hung up before her sister could say another word.

Though her skin was aching for more of Garrett's touch, she knew she would end up making love to him. And she couldn't. Not yet. Not until the promotion race was no longer a strain between them.

"I'd better get going," Garrett said, taking the cue.

As he opened the door, he turned and looked at her, as though he wanted to say something else. Instead, he kissed her on the lips and left.

Garrett raced over to Aunt Rosie's house, knowing he was late. He knew his visit to Elena's had only complicated the situation. His libido was on overdrive after being with her.

As he unlocked his aunt's back kitchen door, he felt frustrated with himself. He'd gone to Elena's to tell her that he had a lead for a double account so she could somehow push faster to get more accounts of her own. But he'd gotten completely caught up in his need for her.

He opened the door to find Aunt Rosie sitting at the kitchen table, looking upset, anxiously sorting through a stack of papers.

"What's wrong, Aunt Rosie?" he asked, concerned.

"The young woman who comes to help me on Saturdays is moving to Colorado in a week," she replied. "I need to get someone else, Garrett, but I can't find the agency number."

"I'll handle it," he said, looking through her pile of bills on the counter. "Here it is."

As he slipped the number into his wallet, his aunt stared at him. "What're you waiting for?" she asked.

"I can't call them now," he explained. "The offices are closed. First thing in the morning I'll make arrangements for a new Saturday caregiver."

"I'm not talking about the agency," his aunt said. "Your perfect woman. When do I get to meet the lady that the dating service picked out for you?"

He glanced away from her intense eyes. "She's not ready for that."

"Her or you?"

"Me," he admitted.

"I thought so," she said. "When's that second date with her?"

"Saturday night," he replied, anxious and excited at the same time about it.

"Good," his aunt said as she got up and turned on the television set. "Garrett, if she's the lady for you, no matter how much you fight it, she'll stay glued to your life. And don't worry, I'll meet her."

She flipped on a marriage game show to try to make her point. But every time he heard the words *happily married,* he felt a pain in his gut that wouldn't go away.

Ten minutes before her afternoon appointment, Elena entered the reception area of Mr. Slater's spacious office on Ventura Boulevard. Her stomach churned with nervousness as she practiced in her mind what she planned to say.

She knew she had to get those two accounts before her meeting with Stanley, which she'd managed to postpone till later that day.

Her legs felt slightly trembly as she walked up to the reception desk. "I'm Elena Martin. I have a two-o'clock appointment with Mr. Slater," she told the receptionist, winding the leather handles of her attaché case until the twisted leather pressed hard into her fingers.

The young woman checked the large appointment book that was lying open on the desk, made a quick call and then said, "Mr. Slater will be with you in a few moments, Ms. Martin."

Elena was too tense to sit down, so she stood near the reception desk, trying to rerun her prepared talk in her head. But she kept thinking about Garrett's surprise visit to her apartment.

She still couldn't get over that he'd stopped by her place because he'd been concerned about her not having any accounts yet. He was worried about her, which made her feel even more connected to him.

As the receptionist talked on the telephone, Elena admired the colorful flowers on the reception desk, remembering the beautiful flowers Garrett had sent for her baseball bruise. Every gesture of his seemed to tell her that he cared for her a lot, even though he hadn't said it in words.

Her gaze wandered to the appointment book lying next to the vase. She saw her name listed for two o'clock. She haphazardly glanced at Mr. Slater's other appointments for the day.

Suddenly her heart momentarily stopped beating. She was sure that she was seeing wrong. But one name kept glaring out at her. Garrett Sims. He'd had a nine-o'clock with Mr. Slater!

"Ms. Martin," the receptionist said, "Mr. Slater is ready to see you."

She could barely hear her. All that was running through her head was that Garrett had already met with the owner of the two luxury buildings. Before her; way before her.

Feeling crushed that he'd beaten her to another account, she could see that the receptionist was waiting for her. How could she go in there after Garrett had already done his sales pitch for the buildings? Yet she couldn't walk out on her appointment, when Mr. Slater had made time to see her.

She took a deep breath and forced herself to enter the owner's spacious office, knowing he was seeing her just to be polite.

"Ms. Martin, my secretary tells me that you visited my two buildings in Westwood," began Mr. Slater, a distinguished man in his late fifties, dressed in a business suit.

"Yes, I did," she replied, filled with turmoil as she sat down in the leather chair near his desk.

"What were your impressions?" he asked.

"Well—" she began, but her voice caught with emotion. She couldn't believe that Garrett could be so cold. "Mr. Slater, I understand that you've already met with—" She stopped. Why should she give up because of Garrett? Feeling a rush of pride at how hard she'd prepared, she decided that she deserved to be heard. She opened her attaché case on her lap.

"If I were the property manager of your two buildings, Mr. Slater," she began with determination, "I would hire top-of-the-line landscapers at low cost. I'd get diligent cleaning personnel to sparkle up the lobbies and hire an efficient elevator service at discount rates." She took out budget sheets. "I've prepared an estimated expense sheet calculating the yearly expenses for each building. I assure you that you would substantially save money with my budget.''

The businessman leaned forward on his desk. ''I'd be very interested in seeing your projected budget.''

''Of course,'' she said, holding back her surprise at his curiosity.

She handed him the expense sheet, fighting the disappointment about Garrett. His visit to her apartment suddenly haunted her. Did he know then that he had the appointment before her? But how could that be? He'd acted like he cared about her. She didn't know what to believe about him anymore.

''Excellent, Ms. Martin, excellent,'' Mr. Slater said. ''I have been looking for these kinds of numbers.'' He picked up his phone. ''Terese, bring me the property management contract.'' Then he arose from his chair and extended his hand. ''You are hired, Ms. Martin. I look forward to Grant Property Management tending to my two apartment buildings.''

Flabbergasted, she shook his hand. ''I'm excited about working with you, Mr. Slater,'' she said, feeling in a daze.

Elena didn't remember signing her name to the contract. She barely remembered leaving the private office and returning to the reception area.

How could she have gotten the account when Garrett had talked to Mr. Slater first? Stunned and confused, she walked up to the receptionist. ''I was wondering,'' she began. ''I noticed Garrett Sims's name on Mr. Slater's schedule book.''

The receptionist glanced at the page. ''Yes, I remember Mr. Sims,'' she replied. ''While he was waiting for his appointment, he glanced at the schedule book. Then he mumbled your name, quickly apologized that he had to cancel his meeting with Mr. Slater and left.''

Elena's mind was whirling as she exited the building.

She couldn't believe it. Garrett had seen that she had a later appointment, and he'd dropped his own appointment and given up his chances for the double account for *her!*

Driving back to the office, she was so thrilled she felt like her tires weren't touching the asphalt-paved street. *Garrett cares about me! He really cares!* That double account would've put him miles ahead of her in the promotion race.

Instead, Garrett had put *her* first.

As she zipped onto the crowded freeway, she couldn't help fantasizing that he was trying to get closer to her. Maybe he really did want to develop a committed relationship with her, just like he'd contracted on the Marriage Connection form.

She felt the sudden urge to drive to the Sherman Oaks office to surprise him. She wanted to tell him that he made her feel treasured by him. And more than anything, she dreamed of asking if he wanted to be in a committed relationship with her as much as she did with him! Instead she drove back to her office.

The moment she entered her office, Grace immediately said that Stanley was waiting to talk to her. With a surge of enthusiasm, she walked into his office.

"Congratulations," Stanley said. "I heard you signed a contract with Ralph Slater to manage his two apartment buildings in Westwood."

"How did you know?" she asked, taken aback.

"I have spies," he replied with a smile, before picking up his ringing telephone.

He asked the person on the line to hold. "I've got to take this call, Elena. Good going on that double account."

"Thanks," she said as she left his office.

She suddenly felt confused. The only person who knew she went to Mr. Slater's office was Garrett. Had he phoned Slater's office to find out if she'd gotten the account and then called Stanley to tell him that he was the one who let her have it by canceling his own appointment?

She hated to think that way. She wanted to believe that Garrett was earnestly building a solid relationship with her.

"Great new account, Elena!" Grace said to her.

"Did Garrett tell everybody in the office?" she blurted, feeling more hurt by the minute.

"Garrett?" the receptionist repeated, confused.

"I thought that he—"

"Not at all," she said. "A few moments before you got to the office, Stanley got a call from the apartment building owner, Ralph Slater, who personally thanked Stanley for sending you over to his office."

"Oh, yes, of course," she stammered, feeling awkward and relieved.

Grace looked at her sideways. "Why did you think Garrett—"

"Don't mind me," she interrupted, hoping she hadn't given Grace a clue that she and Garrett were involved. "I'm just paranoid about Garrett's beating me to the job."

She hurried to her cubicle, realizing that her emotions were completely up and down about Garrett. She knew it was her own fault. She still felt insecure that Garrett might not want a future with her. She wished she could completely trust in her relationship with him. Because, more than ever, she wanted Garrett to be her man.

After work, she stopped at the bakery to buy supersize chocolate chip cookies for her nephews and Jan to celebrate her double-account coup. She wished she could call Garrett to invite him over, too. She knew that was a nutty idea. After all, how could he celebrate her success when he had to worry about his own?

As she drove to her sister's house, she found herself taking the longer route on Olympic Boulevard where she would pass the Santa Monica ball field. She remembered Garrett telling Tod that he played there after work with his friends.

Her stomach felt jittery as she stopped for a red light next to the ball field. She knew she should drive past without looking for him. If he'd wanted her to come to the field, he would've asked her.

Yet she powered open the passenger window to glance at the lit field to her right. Her heart skipped a beat when she saw Garrett.

He was standing near a bench, laughing and talking to his buddies. He wore a baseball cap, beige sweatpants and a T-shirt. He was packing a mitt and bat into his gear bag, ready to leave.

The deafening horn of a semi-trailer truck behind her turned her attention back to driving. She hadn't realized that the light had changed to green.

She saw Garrett turn at the sound, and his eyes met hers. She knew she should smile and then drive off so that she didn't give him the impression that she was chasing after him. She didn't want to scare him away just when he was emotionally moving toward her.

"Elena!" she heard Garrett call out, waving to her.

She should've just waved back and gone to her sister's. On impulse, though, she pulled to the curb.

Her hands felt clammy on the steering wheel as she parked. She realized she wasn't wearing any lipstick, and her hair was every which way. She quickly tried to fluff up the strands.

Calm down, Elena, calm down, she instructed herself. But her inner voice cried back, *I can't! I need Garrett to know that I want him in my life!*

"Garrett, is that Elena in the car?" Trey asked with high interest.

Garrett quickly zippered his gear bag, eager to get to her. "Yeah, that's her," he replied.

"Did you ask her to come by?" his friend pursued.

"No."

"She's hooked on you," Trey commented with a grin. "She keeps looking this way, like she can't wait to be with you."

Garrett grabbed his bag. "I'll be right back." He headed toward her car.

"Come on, admit it," his buddy called out. "You're in a relationship now!"

His friend's words hit a vulnerable chord in him, and he couldn't even hurl back a response. He felt anxious as he walked over to her car, unable to think in permanent terms about his life. Yet he couldn't seem to walk fast enough to be with her.

He set his gear bag on the ground and squatted down at her driver's side window. Elena's lips were bare of lipstick. Her hair was slightly tousled. He held himself back from kissing her, aware that his buddies were watching as they waited near his Mustang, ready to go out for Mexican food.

"You remembered," he said to her.

"About what?" she asked, her blue eyes so vulnerable, so open to him.

"Where I play ball after work."

"I was just passing and—" Then she stopped, leaned toward him and pressed her lips to his. Her kiss got deeper as her tongue blended with his.

Loud hoots and whistles suddenly sprouted from his baseball buddies in the distance.

"I better go," she whispered, and then started up the engine of her car.

Shell-shocked by her kiss, he watched her drive into the Olympic Boulevard traffic.

"Whew!" Trey said from behind him. "What did you say to her to cause that response?"

"Nothing," he replied, still stirred by her mouth on his.

"She's serious about you, very serious," his friend said. "If you're not planning to buy her an engagement ring, I think you better cool it with her."

At the Mexican restaurant, later, he kept pouring the chili sauce over his chicken taco. He was nervous about his second prearranged date with her on Saturday night. Being alone with her would only deepen his feelings for her. How was he going to let her know that she had no future with him?

As he took a big bite of the taco, his mouth went on fire from the chili sauce. He quickly downed an entire glass of water in one gulp, not knowing what to do about his equally hot and fiery feelings for Elena.

Six

When Elena got to her sister's house, she was in such a turmoil about having boldly kissed Garrett in front of his friends that she almost left the cookies she'd bought in the car.

"El, the agency just got me a new Saturday job caring for an elderly lady," Jan said excitedly as the kids grabbed cookies and ran into the living room to play.

"That's terrific," she said, trying to get her mind off her impetuous behavior.

She quickly told Jan about the new accounts and how Garrett had left them for her.

"Wow," Jan responded. "He gave up two accounts for you? You must be in seventh heaven."

She slid into a chair, feeling chaotic inside. "Jan, I'm totally in love with him," she revealed. "I want to be with him all the time. The second I get the chance, I'm kissing him!"

"That's the way a woman in love acts," her sister said.

"But I can't feel that way," she insisted. "Not when I'm fighting him for the promotion. Not when I should be holding back my feelings to protect my opportunity for the job." She stood up, too nervous to sit. "Jan, I'm afraid to go on the second Marriage Connection date with Garrett. How am I going to go to a romantic restaurant with him and pretend I don't love him?"

"You're not going to a public restaurant with him," her sister hesitantly said.

"What do you mean?" she asked, her anxiety level slowly rising.

"Your second date is on a private beach in Malibu," Jan replied, showing her the letter she had received from the service.

Her eyes scanned the note describing a romantic evening on the sand and sea under the moon and stars.

"A secluded beach, just him and me?" she asked, feeling both exhilarated and anxious at the same time.

Before Jan could reply, the kids started arguing in the living room and she had to leave the kitchen to take care of the problem.

Elena stared at the private beach letter, fantasizing about making love to Garrett under the silver moon, and at the same time trying to figure out how she was going to stay out of his arms!

When early Saturday evening arrived, Elena was filled with nervous anticipation as she drove along Pacific Coast Highway.

As per the suggestion of the dating service, she wore a bikini under her clothes. She arrived at the parking lot of a secluded beach on the Malibu shore. There was a white van parked with black lettering on the side saying, Catering Service.

Her breath quickened when she saw Garrett's parked Mustang, knowing he was already on the beach waiting for her.

Under the dusky, terra-cotta sun, she carried her sandals and walked barefoot on the white evening sand toward a broad-striped, black-and-white wind tent in the distance near the shoreline.

She saw a waiter setting down a blanket and two fluffy pillows on the sand. Nearby were two chairs and a small round table covered in white linen, a glass lantern with a flickering candle on top. She could faintly hear a tape player resonating soft jazz music against the background of the crashing waves.

Her heartbeat sped up when she spotted Garrett standing near the water's edge watching the sun slowly set. His cream shirt and beige pants blew in the ocean wind, caressing his solid body.

Her heart filled with love for him. But she couldn't reveal her feelings to him yet. Not until she was completely sure he wanted a life with her.

Just then, Garrett turned around, as though he could sense her watching him. His face lit up when he saw her. Her insides melted.

She impulsively ran toward him on the damp sand. All of her reservations disappeared. Her only desire was to be in his arms. He immediately met her and instantly encased her against his strong body. The world felt totally complete to her.

"Elena," he whispered against her lips.

"I couldn't wait to see you, Garrett," she whispered back, forgetting her vow to control her emotions with him.

Under the moonlight, against the splash of the crashing waves, her mouth met his. His taste, his smell, she felt like she was home.

"Dinner is served," the waiter said.

Flushed and hot from his embrace, she released her arms from around his neck, realizing that she'd just arrived for the date, and she was already in his arms.

Garrett took her hand and led her to the table where he pulled out a chair for her to sit. The candlelight glowed, and the aroma of shrimp scampi, buttered saffron rice and asparagus mingled with the scent of fresh ocean air.

As the waiter placed the white linen napkin on her lap and then Garrett's, he said, "If you need anything during dinner, please let me know. After I serve dessert, I will be leaving the beach and will return one hour later to clean up for the end of your date."

One hour alone with Garrett. She wanted to rush through dinner so the waiter would leave. Yet she felt a flood of anxiety at the thought of being on the private beach with him, knowing how easily she softened being near him, how easily she could forget her need to wait to make love to him.

Dinner was over quickly, and before she knew it, the waiter had poured coffee and served chocolate mousse with whipped cream for dessert. As the minutes passed, she could barely drink her coffee or touch the chocolate mousse. She was intensely aware of Garrett across the table from her. She nervously waited for the waiter to clean up.

About a half hour later, the waiter excused himself and pushed the cart filled with their empty dinner dishes across the sand toward the parking lot.

Her stomach fluttered as she found herself alone on the beach with Garrett. She yearned to return to the passion of his arms.

Garrett was only conscious of the Pacific Ocean breeze blowing strands of streaked blond across Elena's face. He leaned across the table and ran his fingers through her silken tresses. Her pink lips parted as he slid his thumb across her bottom lip.

He couldn't resist her, and he realized that if he sat there a moment longer he'd want to lie on the blanket with her and then—

"Elena, do you want to go for a swim?" he suggested, hoping the ocean water would cool down his body.

"Sounds great," she said, grabbing her bag and taking out a towel.

Wearing his swim trunks under his clothes, he removed his pants and shirt. The ocean sea breeze hit his bare chest and legs like a rush of air-conditioning. His gaze became suddenly riveted to Elena as she began to undress.

She unzipped her skirt, and the fabric fell to the blanket. His eyes lowered to the skimpy royal blue bikini barely concealing her bottom. Her long, shapely, bare legs almost asked to be stroked.

He felt like he was in her bedroom and she was taking off her clothes to go to bed with him.

He took a deep breath of sea air, trying to disengage his sensual fantasy. But then she peeled off her blouse. Her ample breasts almost overflowed the top of her bikini. As she turned and bent over to put her clothes away, his gaze caught the faint strip of fabric between her legs concealing her femininity.

"Elena, I'll race you to the water!" he choked out, unable to handle his desire for her another second.

In the next instant she dashed ahead of him toward the expansive sea, which was glowing with the rays of the silver moon.

"Slowpoke!" she called out, laughing.

"Oh, yeah?" he responded.

He chased after her, and his feet splashed against the cold ocean.

"The water's freezing!" she squealed, then she dove into a wave to get away from him.

He jumped into the swell after her. When he surfaced, he grabbed her around the waist and spun her around to face him.

"I got you," he said, laughing.

"That's because I let you!" she teased back.

Her golden hair was dripping. Her eyes were sparkling. Her wet bikini top was pasted against her heaving breasts. He could see her nipples protruding against the soaked fabric.

Garrett couldn't hold back. He drew her pulsating body to him. His mouth hungrily found hers. The salty water mingled with his kiss.

Just as a wave was about to crash over their heads, he lifted her by the waist above the foam. The water splashed past them to shore. But instead of setting her feet down, he pressed his mouth against her wet swollen mounds.

"Elena, I need you," he whispered as his lips seared each taut nipple beneath the wet bikini top.

A big wave swept into them, almost knocking them off their feet. He held on to her hot body. Her feet were on the ocean floor, and his hands gripped her bikini-covered buttocks, guiding her against his growing masculinity. She groaned against his lips.

Another wave washed over them. "The ocean's getting too rough," she said. "Let's go back to the blanket."

She playfully pushed him into a wall of water and ran toward shore. Surfacing, he saw her glistening shapely body nearing the blanket.

Cool down before it's too late, his mind warned. But as he ran toward her, his body ached with a desire for her that he couldn't control. And his heart yearned to get closer to her.

* * *

Elena tumbled onto the soft dry blanket, out of breath. Though the evening air was chilly, her skin was flaming from Garrett's touch in the ocean. Her breasts throbbed with pleasure from the feel of his mouth.

Dry off and put your clothes on! her inner voice called out. She knew she should quell her intense desire for him until she was sure he wanted a forever relationship with her.

Suddenly Garrett was lying next to her on the blanket. His curly hair was covered with water droplets. His half-naked, muscular body was wet and vital against hers.

He gazed into her eyes as though she was everything to him. She felt like he was everything to her. She slipped her fingers through his moist hair. She ached to share her body, her soul and every detail of her life with him. But she was afraid of giving all of herself before knowing his true feelings about her.

She leaned on her side, touching his cheek and searching his eyes. "Garrett, tell me," she began. "Why did you cancel your appointment with Mr. Slater?"

"Does it matter?" he asked, tenderly gliding his finger along her neck, sending chills down her body.

"Yes, it matters," she replied, finding it difficult to talk as he trailed his finger to the cleavage of her breasts and then lingered at the front hook of her bikini top.

"Why?" he whispered, his voice growing husky as he slowly unhooked her top.

"It's important to me," she whispered as her breasts burst free into his hands.

"I realized I mistakenly made two appointments at the same time," he explained, as he sensually trailed the tip of his finger around her bare nipple.

"You'd never make an error like that," she whispered.

"I wouldn't?" he whispered back with a mischievous grin. "Who says?"

Then his mouth closed over her bare nipple, licking, sucking, causing electrical sensations to course through her limbs.

All of her defenses melted. She momentarily forgot her fear that he might express his love to her and then she'd find out he never wanted a committed relationship in the first place. She wanted to be loved by him, fully, totally.

She caressed the rippling muscles of his bare chest and lightly bit his broad shoulder, causing him to moan in response.

She sucked in her breath as his warm hand slid between her thighs. She instinctively spread her legs a little, wanting him to touch her most private spot. She felt his finger gently brush against the fabric covering her femininity.

Tingles of pleasure flooded through her body. She felt his finger circling, pressing, massaging her pleasure spot over the bikini causing her to spasm against his touch.

She felt close to him, so close to him, and she yearned to feel him inside of her.

The sight of the waiter approaching in the distance put an end to her thoughts. He was pulling a cart, ready to dismantle the paraphernalia of their love date.

"The waiter," she whispered, slipping free of his sturdy arms.

With her skin scalding from his caresses, she quickly put on her bikini top and blouse. She saw Garrett getting dressed, too, but he kept glancing at her with a caring in his eyes that made her want him even more.

As the waiter got nearer to their love site, Elena felt Garrett gently slip his arm around her shoulders, and he kissed her tenderly on the lips.

"Garrett," she whispered, "all I'll be thinking about for the next two weeks is our third date."

"Me, too," he whispered back, pressing her closer to him.

"It seems like forever away," she told him.

Just then, the waiter approached. "Excuse me, Mr. Sims," he said, holding a piece of paper and pen in his hand. "Could you sign the release form that your second date has been completed?"

As Garrett signed the paper, she got her stuff, not wanting to leave him, but knowing she had one more special date with him. She secretly hoped that on their last date, he would make future plans with her so their relationship would be molded permanently together.

Garrett couldn't hurry fast enough to put his signature on the release form. He needed to be alone with Elena. As he walked her to the parking lot and opened her car door for her, he wanted to hold her close to him again.

"I'll drop by the Santa Monica office next week to see you," he heard himself say.

"I can't wait," she told him, kissing him softly on the lips and then driving away.

Torn about his relationship with her, Garrett peeled his Mustang onto the Pacific Coast Highway. He would've made love to her if the waiter hadn't arrived. He wanted to experience that she was part of him for those few minutes.

Yet he knew he could never share the ultimate intimacy with her. Blending mind, body and spirit with her would mean total commitment. A commitment he wasn't ready to give.

Garrett drove straight to Trey's, unable to return to his lonely apartment. He remembered his friend saying that he'd be home watching a videotape if he couldn't get a date for that night.

When he knocked on Trey's door, he was surprised to see his buddy dressed in a pressed shirt and pants instead of shorts and T-shirt. He could hear soft music in the background.

"Trey, do you have a few minutes?" he asked.

"Actually, no," his friend replied, awkwardly glancing back into his apartment. "I've got company."

"Who?"

"Julie," he replied, lowering his voice.

"Your ex-wife, Julie?" Garrett repeated incredulously.

"Yeah."

"I thought you never wanted to see her again," he told him, remembering the night they both vowed to stay single and never get deeply emotionally involved with another woman again.

Trey closed the door a little. "I only have a few seconds to talk," he began. "She's in the bathroom." His eyes warmed. "She called me today. She said she was sorry that we broke up. She asked if she could see me."

"Are you going back with her?" he asked, worried about his friend being hurt again.

"I don't know," he replied unsurely. "But I'm happy to see her, Garrett. I'm glad she's with me right now."

Garrett returned to his apartment, feeling more unsettled than before he saw Trey. He flipped on the TV set, blindly scanning through the channels. He kept thinking about him and Elena. Could it ever work between them?

He flicked off the set and turned on a jazz CD, hoping to quell his troubled thoughts. But the emotion-filled music stimulated his pent-up feelings even more. He wanted to believe that he could have a permanent relationship with Elena. But one question kept looming up in his mind. Would she stay with him for the rest of her life?

He grabbed the telephone and dialed her apartment number. As her telephone rang, he wondered what he'd say to her. *If I married you, would you leave me after a few months, a year, ten years?* He hung up the phone, wishing he could get an answer but knowing he never could.

Sunday afternoon, at the Santa Monica Mall, Elena excitedly walked through a trendy men's clothing store looking for a surprise present for Garrett.

After last night, she almost felt like he was her man. The way he'd kissed her. The way he'd touched her. She was sure he was telling her that he needed her in his life.

Jan joined her in the store. "I've got a few minutes. Tod and Bennie are at a children's storytelling session next door."

"Do you think Garrett might like this wild tie?" she asked, holding up a green and blue geometric style.

Her sister fingered the silk. "El, can I ask you something about Garrett?"

"Sure," she replied, staring at the tie, wanting it to be perfect for him.

"Has Garrett made any future plans with you other than your last Marriage Connection date?" Jan asked.

"Not yet," she replied, feeling uneasy. "But I know he will."

"Are you sure?"

She set down the tie. "Why are you suddenly doubting my relationship with him?" she asked. "You're the one who's been encouraging me to get closer to him."

"I know, I know," Jan went on. "But I'm getting a little worried."

"About what?"

"You're talking about him as though he's almost your fiancé."

"I feel like he almost is," she admitted.

"Has he asked you to meet his family?"

"Well, no," she replied, finding herself leaving the

men's department without buying the tie. "He hasn't discussed his family with me."

Outside, in the crowded mall, Elena walked over to the children's bookstore window. She could see Bennie and Tod sitting on a carpet with other kids listening to an author read aloud her newest children's tale.

"El, I didn't mean to upset you," her sister added. "I don't want you to get your expectations up about Garrett and then—"

"He won't hurt me that way," she quickly said. "I felt so close to him at the beach. I know he felt the same about me."

"Maybe the promotion anxiety is keeping him from opening his entire life to you," Jan said. "I bet when the job thing is settled, he'll start talking about a future with you."

"He will, I know he will," she said, trying to convince herself, trying to push back the doubts looming in her mind.

On Monday at the Sherman Oaks office, Garrett hung up the phone, trying to digest the news he'd gotten from a Realtor who might have a large account for him. But he couldn't focus on business.

He wanted to call Elena to explain that he was all mixed up about his future and that was why he couldn't make any promises to her.

Just then, his telephone rang. "Garrett," Stanley said over the phone, sounding concerned, "are you aware that Elena has caught up to you in the new account area?"

"I heard about it," he replied, knowing he was the one who wanted her to catch up.

"Do you have any potentials on the burner?"

"I might have something big cooking."

"I hope so," his boss said. "Because if Elena tops you, I'm obligated to give the vice presidency to her."

His stomach tightened, knowing how hard he'd been working toward getting that job. "I'll move faster on it, Stan."

"I'm counting on you," his boss said. "I'll be out of the office this afternoon. I'll check with you tomorrow."

When Garrett hung up, he felt a tension in him that was almost unbearable. He'd sacrificed the two luxury apartment buildings because of his feelings for Elena. With that account under his belt, he would've been almost guaranteed the promotion.

He grabbed his jacket, not wanting to waste any time pursuing the account he'd heard about. Yet he couldn't budge from the office.

Something deep inside of him wanted to pull back his efforts. He didn't want to squash Elena's chances for the promotion. Yet he wanted his goal of eventually running Stanley's company to become a reality. He felt crushed in the middle.

His telephone rang. The tenant who owed back rent was on the line. He thanked Garrett over and over for not evicting him and his family. He got a job, and he'd get the rent money to Garrett tomorrow morning.

Feeling like he'd done at least one thing right, Garrett headed out of the office to check out the new account possibility. However, as he drove he found himself turning off toward the Santa Monica office. He had to see Elena, even for just a few seconds. Stanley had told him he'd be out for the afternoon, so he felt halfway safe going there.

As he walked into the office, he ran through his head the reasons he'd give to whoever asked as to why he was dropping by. He nodded to the junior property managers.

"Garrett, how are you?" Grace asked.

"Just fine," he replied. "Is Stan in?"

His pulse pounded when he saw Elena in the file room busily looking through a stack of charts.

"No, Garrett, he's out for the rest of the day," the receptionist replied.

"Could you tell him I came by?" he asked and then added, "While I'm here, I think I'll check a file on a property Stanley mentioned to me. Are all the charts in the file room?"

"What's the property address?" Grace asked. "I'll get it for you."

"No, thanks, I can do it," he insisted.

Keeping a businesslike attitude, he headed toward the file room. "Hello, Elena, how's it going?" he said, greeting her in a very platonic tone for the office to hear.

Her surprised eyes met his. "Everything's fine, just fine, Garrett," she replied in an equally businesslike voice. But then in a whisper, she asked, "What are you doing here?"

"To see you," he whispered back, and in a co-worker voice said, "The chart I'm looking for is in the file cabinet behind the door. Do you mind if I close it to get to the drawer?"

"Sure, go ahead," she stammered.

He quietly locked the file room door. He leaned against it, staring at her, taking in every inch of her. He wanted to tell her about his life confusion, but he was hesitant. He wasn't sure if she'd immediately lose interest in him. He couldn't stand it if that happened.

Her cheeks grew pink from his bold gaze. "You're crazy coming here."

"I couldn't let today go by without seeing you," he admitted.

"Garrett, you've been on my mind so much that I misfiled two charts and still can't find them!"

Aware of the few precious moments he had with her, he slipped his hands around her small waist and drew her softness to him.

"Garrett, what if someone—"

A moment later she circled her arms around his neck and pressed her mouth to his, ignoring her own question.

Her passion surprised him. She planted sweet kisses on his lips, his eyes and his cheeks with such feeling that he knew he couldn't bring up his commitment hesitancy.

Her tongue danced with his as though she were making love to him. He slipped his hands under the back of her blouse to touch her bare flesh. As he pressed her breasts against his chest, he heard a knock at the door.

"Garrett, did you locate the file you wanted?" Grace called out.

"Yes, Grace, I found exactly what I was searching for," he responded, staring at Elena, referring to his feelings for her.

She whispered, "You better get out of here. If Grace senses something and tells Stanley—"

He could see the worry lines creasing her face. He was making her nervous. He didn't want to do that.

"You're right," he said, quietly unlocking and opening the file room door. In a businesslike voice, he said, "Elena, thanks so much for your help."

"Anytime, Garrett," she replied, her eyes gleaming from their secret moment together.

Garrett's emotions were in an uproar as he left the office. Elena was drawing even closer to him, and he was to her. Yet, his resistance to promising her a future relationship plagued him more than ever.

In his Mustang, he knew he should go to see the Realtor who had the details of the potential new account for him, but he felt like he'd be disloyal to Elena if he went. So he decided to put it off a little while longer.

He zoomed his car to the singles-only apartment building in Palms to check the plumbing work, hoping to get his mind off his confused emotions.

At the apartment complex, he was talking to the plumbing vendor about the final pipe replacements, making sure there'd be no leak problems, when his cell phone buzzed.

"Garrett, this is Sam McGrath," the owner said. "Everything A-okay with the pipe work?"

"Looks fine to me, Sam," he told the owner. "We even came in below budget."

"Excellent," he said. "I'm sure there won't be any leaks in your new apartment."

"My apartment?"

"The tenant in twenty-eight is moving out on Friday," the owner went on. "Your singles pad will be ready for occupancy this weekend."

Singles pad. He felt like a boulder had fallen on his chest.

"Great, Sam," he uttered. "Thanks for looking out for me. I'll start packing my stuff."

As he flipped close the cell phone, he felt a rush of anxiety. He wanted to instantly call the owner back. To tell him what? That he was all mixed up about moving into the singles-only apartment now that Elena had entered his heart? That he'd committed to a two-year lease when he wasn't even sure what was going to happen next week?

Garrett told the plumber he'd talk to him later and headed toward his car. His emotions were chaotic. He needed to focus on the account. He had to keep his goal to head up Stanley's company at the top of his mind.

Seven

At her office Elena hung up the phone in a panic. She'd just gotten a call from the mortgage banker of her sister's house. She'd forgotten to pay Jan's mortgage!

She immediately made a telephone money transfer from her bank account to pay the overdue mortgage. She'd never been lax about helping her sister before.

However, for the past few days she'd been struggling with her emotions about Garrett. She had deliberately not called him. She knew how vulnerable she got talking to and being with him. She needed to keep her distance, just for a little while, so she could be strong enough to search for new accounts since Stanley would be making his decision soon.

She quickly called realty offices in downtown Los Angeles she'd never contacted before. She wished she didn't need the vice president's salary, not if it meant she could lose Garrett. But her sister needed her help for at least six months, maybe even a year, to financially catch up.

"Elena, can you watch the phones while I go to the ladies' room?" Grace asked, peeking into her cubicle, interrupting her turbulent thoughts.

"Sure," she replied, hurrying to the reception desk, which was right near Stanley's office.

As Elena answered the ringing telephones, she could hear Stanley talking on his private line.

"Darn right I'd like that account," he said, his voice rising with interest.

Her ears perked up when she heard the word *account*. She leaned closer to his office door.

"I thought Nathan Franklin's company managed the three Golden Savings Bank buildings in downtown L.A.," he said.

She didn't hear any more details, because a bunch of calls came in for her to answer. She quickly jotted down the name of the buildings that Stanley had spoken about. Her big chance had arrived.

If the bank buildings were available for management, she was determined to impress Stanley by getting that contract for him.

The moment Grace returned, she hurried to her desk and immediately called the main office of the banks, got the number of the owner, Mr. Weston, and connected with his office administrator.

Elena was elated to confirm that the three bank buildings *were* available for management! But when she asked for an appointment, she was told that Mr. Weston would be out of town until next Tuesday and had meetings scheduled for the day of his return.

After Elena practically begged to see him, the woman suggested she drop by the office right before closing time at six o'clock on Tuesday, and maybe she could catch him.

Filled with enthusiasm, she quickly dialed Garrett's cellular number to tell him about her potential success. She immediately hung up. *I can't share my excitement with Garrett,* she told herself. *He's my opponent. He's my rival for the promotion!*

She hated having to shut off her feelings with him whenever it had to do with her career.

More and more she wished there was no promotion at all.

As Garrett carried his black leather sofa into the living room of his singles-only apartment with Trey's help, he inwardly fought every step. The new telephone was hooked up. The refrigerator was in. He was all settled, except for his messed-up emotions.

"Garrett, you're in single man's heaven," Trey said as he glanced out the front window. "Look at those three gorgeous ladies sunbathing by the pool."

"Right," he muttered as he grabbed a soda from the refrigerator.

"What's with you?"

"Maybe I made a mistake moving here."

"What're you talking about?" his friend asked. "You've been waiting for this place for who knows how long."

"Yeah, I guess."

"You guess?"

Feeling conflicted, he put down the soda can and began unpacking the boxes in the living room. "I don't know what I feel anymore."

Just then the telephone rang, and Trey grabbed it before Garrett got a chance. "Julie!" he said into the phone and then turned to Garrett. "I gave her your new number when I got here this morning."

Garrett went into the bedroom to give Trey some privacy. As he began unpacking boxes, he could barely remember why he'd rented this apartment. He knew part of him wanted to fulfill his need to remain single. But drumming at his heart was Elena. He couldn't deny that his bond with her was growing stronger every day.

"Garrett, I've gotta split," Trey said from the bedroom doorway. "I'm going to be with—"

"Julie?" he finished for him.

"Yeah," his friend replied. "I feel like everything I do is just passing time until I see her."

Garrett blindly removed CDs from a box, unable to deny that he felt that way, too, about Elena.

"Trey, have you changed your mind about getting married again?" he couldn't help but ask.

"A few weeks ago, before Julie slammed back into my life," Trey replied, "I would've said a whopping 'no way.'"

"And now?"

His friend mischievously grinned. "Who knows? I might surprise myself."

After Trey left, Garrett yearned to be with Elena. But he knew he'd complicate matters between them with the promotion race so close to the finish line. He had to wait until their last prearranged date.

He grabbed his jacket to get some fast food for dinner, feeling lonelier than he'd felt since his marriage broke up.

On Tuesday, at the apartment complex that Elena managed in West Los Angeles, she anxiously checked the wrought iron security gate she had installed at the owner's request.

She quickly glanced at her watch, nervous about meeting Mr. Weston.

She was still dying inside to call Garrett but had stopped herself a zillion times, afraid she might leak out about the bank buildings.

She turned on her cell phone and called her office to tell Grace that she wouldn't be returning for the rest of the day.

"Elena, are you onto a new account?" the receptionist whispered on the line.

She knew she could trust Grace and couldn't hold in her excitement any longer. "I'm going after an account that Stanley wants," she confided. She explained that she was going directly to the office of the owner of the three Golden Savings Bank buildings in downtown Los Angeles. "If my sister calls, can you tell her where I'll be?"

"Sure, Elena," Grace replied. "I know you'll get that account. I can already see the vice president logo on your new office door!"

"Grace, I needed that!" she said.

She finished her work at the apartment complex earlier than expected and realized that she had an hour before she might catch Mr. Weston.

Filled with nervous energy, she found herself impulsively calling the Sherman Oaks branch to see if Garrett was still there. The secretary, Delia, told her that she and everyone in the office were leaving for the day. But Garrett was on the phone with Stanley, and he had told her that he'd be staying for another hour or so to make a few more calls.

Without leaving her name, Elena said goodbye, hopped into her car and got on the freeway. She knew she'd promised herself not to see or talk to him until their last Marriage Connection date, but she couldn't hold out any longer.

Hopefully, by the time she got there, the entire staff would be gone. Then she could be alone with him for a few precious moments.

Garrett pressed the telephone tight against his ear so he couldn't mistake what Stanley was telling him.

"Garrett, the huge account you just got put you on top," Stanley said from his car phone. "As far as I'm concerned, it looks like the vice president position is yours."

"What about Elena?" he blurted, without thinking. "We've still got another week to hear what she's got."

"You're right," his employer responded. "I'll keep my word and won't make my final decision until the time period is over. But I still feel like I'm talking to the man who will eventually head up my company."

The moment he heard Stanley hang up his car phone, Garrett dialed the Santa Monica branch. He felt compelled to warn Elena that she had to solicit more accounts right away. He needed to feel that Stanley's final decision would be a fair one.

From the corner of his eye, he noticed that Delia had left the office, forgetting her wallet on her desk. He remembered how upset she'd been all day because everyone was pointing out the errors she was making in her work. He placed her wallet in the top drawer of his desk to lock up for protection.

When the phone was answered at the Santa Monica office, Garrett expected to hear Grace's voice, but instead a junior property manager picked up his call, saying that Grace had already left.

"Can I speak to Elena?" he quickly asked.

"I'm sorry, but Elena's not here," the woman said.

"Do you know where she might be?" he said anxiously.

"Let me see if Grace left any messages from Elena on her desk," she replied. "There's a note for Elena's sister, in case she calls, saying that Elena went downtown to speak to the owner of the Golden Savings Bank buildings before closing time at six o'clock."

Garrett didn't remember hanging up the phone. Feeling

numb inside, he stared at the pamphlet of the three Golden Savings Bank buildings lying on his desk. The pamphlet he'd just gotten from the meeting he'd had with Mr. Weston, the owner of the bank buildings. The meeting where he'd signed the contract to manage all three bank buildings. That was why Stanley had called to say he was so high on choosing him as vice president.

Garrett anxiously ran his fingers through his hair, knowing Elena was on her way to try to get that account. He anxiously paced the office, wondering what to do. He had to contact her before she arrived at Weston's office. But he dreaded telling her that the account she was going after was now his.

Elena excitedly opened the front door to the Sherman Oaks branch, hoping everyone in the office had already gone.

"Delia, I found your wallet—" she heard Garrett say and then stop when he saw her enter.

For a moment she thought she saw a streak of panic in his eyes.

"Garrett," she began in a low voice, "did everyone leave?"

"Yes," he replied. "Nobody's here except me."

She was so happy to see him that she circled her arms around his neck. "I can't stay for long," she said. "I'm on my way downtown on business." She saw his jaw tense, and she wondered if she'd done the right thing dropping by his office without calling him first. Maybe he was in the middle of pursuing an account. "I hope you don't mind that I came," she added.

"Mind?" he replied. "No, absolutely not. I'm glad you're here."

She tightened her arms around his neck. "I feel so free

being with you in the office without worrying about Stanley.''

"Elena," he began, "about that business thing you're going to—"

She put her finger to his lips. "No work talk."

"But I need to tell you—"

She kissed him before he could finish. She felt his hands gently press on her back, nudging her body closer to him. She could feel his heart pumping hard against her breasts.

She didn't want to leave. She wanted to spend the evening with him. But she had to get to the bank building account.

"Garrett," she murmured, gently releasing her lips from his. "I better get going."

His arms remained around her. His eyes looked troubled.

"Elena, wait," he said.

"Garrett, what's wrong?" she asked.

She glanced at her watch. She had fifteen minutes before she could catch Mr. Weston. It would take her twelve minutes to get there.

"The account you're after," he began, his voice strained.

"I wish I could tell you about it, but I can't," she said. "I hate the secrecy between us about accounts, but I don't know what else to do."

As she glanced at her watch again, her eyes caught a pamphlet lying on the desk near them. The desk with Garrett's name stand on it.

Elena felt the breath knocked out of her as she picked up the pamphlet with the photo and address of the three Golden Savings Bank buildings.

"Elena, I tried to tell you—"

"You met with Mr. Weston?" she forced out, biting her bottom lip so hard she could almost taste blood.

"I got the account this morning," he said in a low voice. "When I found out from your office that you were going to see Weston—"

"Garrett, you don't need to explain." Feeling totally defeated, but not daring to show him, she set the pamphlet back on his desk. "I really need to go."

Crushed inside she headed toward the closed door, feeling tears blurring her eyes but fighting to hold back until she was out of his sight.

Suddenly she felt Garrett grab her hand. "Elena—"

"There's nothing more to say," she choked out. She wanted to be angry with him. She wanted to tell him that he'd taken away the account that would've put her on top with Stanley, but his eyes were filled with as much anguish as she felt inside.

"Elena, I can't stand knowing I'm the one causing you pain," he said. "I'll stop going after accounts for as long as you want so you can have a fair chance to catch up."

"No, Garrett, it wouldn't be fair to you," she said, her defenses melting with his every word.

"I'd never hurt you, Elena, never," he said, his voice filled with emotion. "I'll do anything to make you happy."

"Oh, Garrett!" she said. "All I care about is you, too!"

She pressed her lips to his, and he hungrily kissed her back. He drew her body tightly to his, as though he couldn't get close enough to her.

His hands clasped around her waist and then he lifted her up on the desktop, his mouth never leaving hers. She felt his hands gently touch her thighs, slowly pushing up her skirt, sending shivers of pleasure through her.

Suddenly the office door swung open. Through a haze of sensual reverie, Elena saw a young woman standing at the opened door. She saw Garrett's eyes dart in the same direction as he released his hands from her body.

"Delia," he said in a strained voice.

"I—I forgot my wallet," the secretary uncomfortably told him.

"I know, I saw it on your desk and put it in my drawer for protection," he said, helping Elena down. "I was— we were—you know Elena Martin from the Santa Monica branch, don't you?"

Elena felt her cheeks flaming. "I'm sure I've talked to you over the phone."

"Yes, of course," the young woman awkwardly said.

"Delia, I'll get your wallet," Garrett told her.

Elena grabbed her bag. "Have a good evening, Garrett," she heard herself utter. "You, too, Delia."

When she reached her car, she was out of breath, aware that the secretary had seen her and Garrett embracing, against Stanley's office policy.

She should've been freaked out. She should've been frightened out of her head that her job might be threatened.

Instead, as she got in her car, all she could hear were Garrett's words in her mind, *I'd never hurt you, Elena, never.* She didn't care about the bank buildings. She didn't care that he was way ahead of her with new accounts. She was too filled with exhilaration that he'd opened his heart to her.

Excited about how close she felt to him, she fantasized about his wanting to be with her way after the Marriage Connection date was over. She was so caught up in her fantasy that she nearly missed her exit off the freeway.

She quickly drove to the Santa Monica Mall to shop for a new outfit for her third date. A few days ago her sister had received a notice from the dating service indicating that the last prearranged date would be an all-day rendezvous on Catalina Island.

She checked out every trendy shop at the mall, searching for the most exquisite casual clothing ensemble she could find. She had to look stunning for Garrett. She wanted their final Marriage Connection date to be so special that he'd never want to be apart from her again.

At a fashionable department store, she bought a salmon-colored midriff top, white miniskirt and a matching salmon sweater with mother-of-pearl buttons.

Then she went to the men's department and found the geometric-patterned tie she'd wanted to buy Garrett when she'd been with her sister. Now she felt ready to give him the gift from her heart, knowing almost positively that Garrett would be with her forever.

In the evening, as Garrett parked in front of Trey's apartment building, he was distraught with worry about Delia telling someone that she'd seen Elena with him at the office. He knew Delia was concerned about losing her job, and he hoped she'd be too busy trying to hold on to it to care.

Garrett walked toward his friend's apartment wishing that Trey hadn't insisted that he hurry over to his place. He needed to be alone. Being with Elena at his office had totally whirled him around. Tender feelings for her were pulling at his heart. He realized that his desire for her was stronger than he could control.

He couldn't believe that he'd offered to halt all efforts to get new accounts so she could accumulate more of her own.

What's going on with me? he silently asked himself. He was temporarily putting aside the career he was diligently trying to establish. All for Elena. He couldn't seem to stop himself from putting her feelings first at every turn.

As he rang Trey's doorbell, he felt a tornado of emotion between his need for Elena and what he thought were his life priorities.

"Come on in, Garrett," Trey called out behind the closed door.

When he opened the door, he stopped when he saw Trey packing a suitcase. "Where are you going?"

His buddy grinned. "On my honeymoon."

"You got married?" he asked, stunned.

"Just about," his friend replied. "Julie and I plan to have a quick ceremony performed on Friday morning."

"I can't believe it," he forced out. "I thought you were going to play it cautious. I thought—"

"Garrett, she's half my heart," Trey cut in. "Every time I try imagining the rest of my life without her, I feel lost inside."

Garrett stood there speechless. He felt in a turmoil because that was the way he was beginning to feel about Elena.

"So, Garrett, will you be my best man at the Santa Monica Courthouse this Friday to witness our vows?" Trey asked. "I couldn't get married a second time without you there giving me luck."

"I wouldn't miss it," he replied, shaking his buddy's hand.

As Garrett drove to his apartment, he kept telling himself that Trey's circumstance was different from his with Elena. His friend had been married to Julie before. He knew her patterns, habits and vulnerabilities, and she knew his. He was sure his friend would be able to sense if Julie wanted out of their second marriage, and maybe his buddy could prevent the disaster from happening again.

With Elena, how could Garrett be sure that her feelings

for him wouldn't change once she was living with him, day after day, just like his ex-wife's had.

His muscles felt tense as he entered his singles apartment. He admired Trey for taking the risk again with Julie. He just wasn't sure if he could do the same.

Friday morning, in the judge's chambers at the Santa Monica Courthouse, Garrett stood next to his best friend during the marriage ceremony. He listened as the judge read the marriage vows to Trey and Julie.

When he heard the spiritual words, "Until death do us part," he wondered if those eternal words could ever apply to him and Elena. Doubts loomed up in his mind. Doubts about his ability to sustain an everlasting marriage. Doubts that wouldn't go away.

At the West Los Angeles commercial building that she managed, Elena checked to make sure that the faulty air-conditioning system was being properly repaired.

She could hardly concentrate. She wanted to give Garrett the tie she'd bought for him. The beautifully wrapped box was in her car, waiting for the perfect time. The gift was her way of letting him know that she felt like he was her man.

After handling the problem, she grabbed her briefcase, containing the list of realty companies in Beverly Hills she planned to visit.

She felt more pressure than ever to get accounts after Garrett had promised to let her catch up. She knew it was hard for him to pull back, and she knew he was doing it just for her.

As she waited at the elevator, a familiar voice called out, "Elena Martin?"

Her ex-boss, Nathan Franklin, walked over. Nathan, in his mid-sixties, owned the property management firm she used to work for prior to getting the job with Stanley.

"Nathan, what's new?" she asked, shaking his hand, feeling anxious that her time was running out to get more accounts.

"I'm moving to New York with my wife and three kids," he replied. "I want to sell my property management firm, and I'm looking for a buyer."

A kaleidoscope of lights went off in her head. "Nathan, how many accounts would be part of the deal?" she quickly asked.

"I've got twelve apartment and eight commercial buildings under contract."

"Twenty?" she blurted, so excited that she could burst. "Nathan, with the right price, I might have a buyer for you!"

After going to Nathan's office to talk, Elena jet-propelled her car back to her office. She had a list of every property that Nathan's company managed and the incredible selling price she'd negotiated with him. She wished she could instantly call Garrett. She knew he'd be proud of her business possibility.

She was so excited that, before asking Grace if Stanley could see her, she burst into his office.

"What's the emergency, Elena?" Stanley asked, surprised. "Do you have a new account for me?"

"Not one, Stanley," she told him. "How about twenty new accounts!"

In a burst of energy, she told him about the sale price she'd negotiated for Nathan Franklin's business, if Stanley was interested. Her hand was trembling as she showed him the extensive list of lucrative commercial and apartment accounts.

"That company is a gold mine," he said. "And the price would be a steal." A satisfied grin crossed his face. "Elena, you did great. You did just great."

Stanley immediately called Nathan on the telephone to

confirm the price and told him that his attorney would call about the business arrangements.

When he hung up the phone, he looked at her, impressed, very impressed. "I'll be honest with you, Elena," he confided. "Right from the start, I was considering Garrett over you as vice president of my company."

She swallowed. "And now?"

He leaned forward on his desk, just as his telephone started ringing. "You just proved yourself to be a top contender," he replied. "I'm going to have a very difficult time making a choice. I'll need a little more time to think about it."

Overwhelmed with joy, she felt like hugging him, but he answered his telephone, and she left his office feeling like she was hovering two feet off the ground.

At her desk, she couldn't wait to tell her sister. She blindly dialed Jan's work number, eager to share her success. The line was busy, and she pressed the redial button.

"Hello?" Garrett's voice echoed in her ear.

She realized she'd accidentally dialed his number instead! The sound was staticky, and she knew he was riding in his car.

"Garrett," she said, realizing she was talking to the man who mattered most in her life but whose career would be hurt by her great accomplishment. "I called because—because I just wanted to say hello!"

"Congratulations," he told her.

Her body tensed. "For what?"

"I just hung up with Stanley."

She bit her bottom lip. "Did he tell you about—" She couldn't even say the words.

"What a feat," he told her. "You've given me a monumental challenge to follow."

"Garrett, I didn't mean—"

"Don't worry about it."

"But I do!"

She needed to know if her success had hurt her relationship with him.

Just then, a barrage of cellular static hit her ear. "Elena, I've got to go," Garrett quickly said, before she was disconnected. "I've got a meeting at Farrow's Café in Century City in fifteen minutes." She could hear in his voice that he was upset but was trying not to show her. "I'll talk to you later."

She hung up feeling an avalanche of emotion. She wanted to feel happy about her unbelievable feat, but she'd stepped way ahead of Garrett after he'd held off pursuing accounts for her.

She couldn't focus on the paperwork on her desk. She wanted to immediately give Garrett the gift she'd picked out. She needed to show him that she cared about him above everything else. She grabbed her bag, determined to see him.

As Garrett parked his car in the underground structure of the Century City Plaza, his feelings were chaotic. He'd wanted to make Elena feel happy about the business deal she'd gotten for Stanley, but instead, he felt like he'd upset her.

Yet the frustration he felt at his dilemma with Stanley was overwhelming. On the phone Stanley had told him outright that if he didn't come up with a biggie account, Elena would be picked instead of him.

As he entered Farrow's Café, he greeted the owner of a commercial building in Manhattan Beach and proceeded to discuss business.

After twenty minutes of talk, Garrett realized that he wasn't getting the account. The businessman decided to save the money he'd spend hiring a management firm and instead have an employee at his own office handle the building.

Garrett was about to leave the booth of the café, feeling more anxiety than ever, when he saw Elena walk in.

"Garrett, I was hoping I'd catch you," she said, out of breath as she slid into the booth beside him. "I feel so guilty about the accounts I just got."

"Don't be," he told her. "You did a superb job."

She looked at him with upset eyes. "What about you?"

He wanted to tell her that he felt like he was drowning, but how could he. She'd blame herself. That was the last thing he wanted.

"I'm doing great," he forced out.

The doubt in her eyes told him that she didn't believe him. "I brought a surprise for you." She handed him a wrapped box. "I hope you like it."

He hesitantly pushed aside the tissue paper. When he saw the colorful tie she'd handpicked for him, a lump formed in his throat. She was giving him a gift, not because it was his birthday or Christmas, but because she cared.

"I could return it, if it's not your style," she quickly said.

"Elena, the tie is perfect," he said.

He took off the tie he was wearing and put on the one she gave him. He never wanted to take it off.

Her blue eyes clouded. "I'm so glad you like it," she said, resting her hand on his leg. "I wish we didn't have to go back to work right away."

His loins stirred at the touch of her palm on his thigh. "Me, too," he said. He wanted to spend the rest of the day with her, naked in bed.

Before he could act further on his feelings, his cell phone rang.

"Garrett, I better go," she said, lightly kissing him on the lips. Then she hurried out of the café.

He quickly answered his phone. "Garrett, I might have

a whopper deal for you," Bert said over the line. "Get over to my office as soon as you can."

"I'm on my way," he said, hanging up.

As he headed for his car, he glanced down at the tie Elena had given him. Everything she did made him feel closer and closer to her.

That was what scared him the most. The more he needed her in his life, the more painful it would be if she wanted to break up with him. He knew he couldn't wait much longer to let her know his resistance to making future plans.

In the optometrist's waiting room, as Elena sat with Jan, Bennie and Tod for Bennie's eye appointment, she excitedly glanced through a bride's magazine.

"Jan, look at this white lace gown," she said, showing her sister.

"It's beautiful," Jan said a bit hesitantly. "El, how do you think Garrett will feel if Stanley gives the vice president job to you and not him?"

She put down the magazine. "Maybe it won't matter to him," she said, knowing she was talking dream words.

"El—" her sister began worriedly.

"I don't want my relationship with him to ever end," she said. And before she knew it, the words came flowing out, "Jan, I love Garrett. I want to marry him."

"How can you?" her sister asked in a worried tone. "You can't become vice president *and* marry Garrett while you're still working at Grant Property Management."

Just then, the nurse called Bennie in for his eye examination. While Elena waited with Tod, she anxiously tried to figure out how she could have the job *and* Garrett, wishing she didn't have to give up one for the other.

* * *

Garrett firmly shook hands with the two co-owners of five commercial buildings in the San Fernando Valley. He felt totally relieved that he'd just signed a contract to manage their properties.

To top it off, the businessmen promised to set up appointments for him to meet with their business associates who also had buildings in the Valley needing management.

As Garrett drove to his aunt's house for a visit, his dream of eventually running Stanley's company suddenly seemed vitally alive again.

He smoothed down the silk tie that Elena had given him. He felt like her gift had brought him the luck he needed.

Why fool himself? He could no longer hide the truth. He was very much in love with Elena. Every time he was with her, he never wanted to part. Yet he knew she was waiting for him to discuss their future together.

Future. Marriage. He pushed his foot down on the accelerator, feeling so much anxiety that he couldn't think straight.

He was so filled with turmoil that when he entered Aunt Rosie's house he realized he'd forgotten to buy the pint of French vanilla ice cream she'd asked him to pick up.

"Aunt Rosie, I'm sorry," he told her. "I'll go out and get the ice cream right now."

"Don't bother, Garrett," his aunt said, sitting in the living room, holding a large magnifier, trying to read the newspaper. "When a man's in love, he forgets stuff."

He nervously ran his fingers through his hair. He couldn't hide his feelings from his aunt. He felt the urge to ask her whether she thought Elena might accept his hesitancy to get married, but he couldn't. He needed to deal with it on his own.

Aunt Rosie put down the newspaper. "My eyesight is

going for sure," she said. "I can barely see the print. But I did find something for you, Garrett. Grab that stack of papers over there."

He handed them to her, his mind still in chaos. "What did you find?"

"Remember when you signed that dating service agreement, and I lost the first page?" she asked. "Well, I found it mixed up with some old newspapers."

As she handed him the sheet, Garrett felt a flood of tension when he saw the letterhead that read, "Marriage Connection." "Are you sure this is the contract I signed?" he anxiously asked.

"That's it."

He couldn't breathe as his gaze locked on one paragraph. "The only requirement is a commitment to want to get married."

He couldn't believe that he'd signed a contract stating that he *wanted* to get married! He put down the paper, feeling like his insides were about to burst. "I'll get that ice cream for you," he told his aunt.

He went outside and leaned against the oak tree in the front yard, breathing in the fresh air, trying to get some oxygen into his lungs.

All this time Elena thought he wanted to get married!

He got into his car, realizing that every gentle word he whispered to her, every passionate caress of her body, was an affirmation of his desire to make a lifelong commitment to her.

Feeling a ton of pressure in his chest, he drove to the ice cream store. He had to tell her that he hadn't known the name of the dating service, that he'd never meant to deceive her about getting married. He needed to tell her about his failed marriage so she'd understand why he could never make that mistake twice.

He knew he'd promised his aunt that he'd never reveal

that she signed him onto the dating service. But he was sure she'd understand why he had to tell Elena.

What tortured him the most was knowing that once he expressed his true feelings about marriage to Elena, he knew he'd lose her forever.

As he entered the ice cream store to order, he was in such a frenzy that he forgot what kind of ice cream his aunt wanted.

Eight

Elena's stomach was filled with butterflies as she sat in her sister's car on the way to her third date.

She could see San Pedro Harbor in the distance where the public charter boat was docked. She held her breath, thinking that in a few minutes she'd be on the boat with Garrett for a romantic day trip to Catalina Island—her last prearranged date with the man she loved.

As Jan drove, she silently hoped that Garrett would talk about his vision for the two of them. Because she already knew hers.

"Aunt Elena, can I go on the boat with you?" Bennie asked from the back seat of the station wagon.

"Benneee, you're so dumb!" Tod said. "Aunt Elena's going on a date with Garrett. She doesn't need you around."

"You, neither!" Bennie responded.

"That's enough, you two," her sister warned as she

drove the car into the parking lot. "El, do you see Garrett? I'm dying to meet him."

Elena saw the charter boat with passengers boarding. She looked for Garrett but didn't see him.

"He's not here yet," she nervously said.

"What're you waiting for?" Jan asked. "Go find him and get on that boat! We'll be waiting for you right here when you return at six o'clock tonight."

She nervously grabbed her bag and left the station wagon. As she walked toward the charter boat, she suddenly felt a chill as the cool morning breeze hit her bare skin under the midriff blouse and miniskirt.

When she reached into her bag to grab her sweater, she realized that she'd left it in the car.

"Jan, my sweater!" she called out, whirling around, but her sister had already driven away.

She suddenly felt Garrett's hand slip around her waist. "Don't worry, Elena," he said, drawing her close to him. "I'll keep you warm."

As his warm fingers gently squeezed the bare flesh of her waistline, tingles cascaded down her body. "I feel toasty already," she said, feeling an instant flow of heat from his body to hers.

The boat horn sounded, calling passengers to board. A surge of happiness rushed through her as she ran with him to the charter boat for the date she hoped would lead to an endless future with him.

As Garrett sat on a bench on the outer deck of the boat with Elena snuggled close to him, his mind reeled with tumultuous thoughts. How was he going to tell her that when he signed the Marriage Connection agreement, marriage wasn't on his mind? That he was hurt so badly in his prior marriage, everything inside of him was fighting against trying it again.

He felt so anxious about telling her, he could barely hear the waves slapping against the side of the ship. He faintly heard the weather being announced on a passenger's radio, predicting a possible thunderstorm later in the day.

Somehow he had to find the right moment to talk to her.

As the boat sped through the vast Pacific Ocean toward Catalina Island, a wave hit the front of the ship and lightly sprayed them.

He gently wiped a sprinkle of ocean water from the tip of her nose. Her eyes were steady on his. Her full lips were colored in raspberry. He wanted to kiss her, but didn't think he had the right because of what he had to tell her.

"Elena, do you want to go inside to stay dry?" he asked.

"Oh, no," she quickly said, turning to face him on the bench. "The spray feels good."

He noticed that her skirt had climbed up her thighs, revealing her bare ivory flesh. He ached to touch her leg and feel the warmth of her skin. But he couldn't allow himself to get that close to her.

When she rested her head against his chest, he was sure she could hear his heart thumping like a war drum—not just because her body was so near his, but because he was sure she would shut tight to him the moment he told her the truth about his hesitation about marriage.

The moment the boat docked at the town of Avalon on Catalina Island, she excitedly asked, "Where should we go first? The souvenir shops? Tour the Catalina Mansion? Go on a quiet walk in the mountains?"

"Whatever you want," he said, squeezing her hand, savoring what might be the last time she'd want to be close to him.

"I don't care what we do," she responded. "I'm just happy being with you."

She was looking at him with such openness, such caring that his heart wrenched. He didn't dare say the words he knew would hurt her.

"Hey, folks," called the bus driver. "We've got two seats left on the tour to the Catalina Mansion."

Elena's eyes lit up. "Want to?"

"If you do."

"Come on!" She kept her hand in his and led him to the two seats at the rear of the bus where they could be alone.

As the bus drove up the hillside of Avalon Canyon Road toward the Catalina Mansion, Garrett was only aware of Elena. She held his arm as she glanced out the open window, as though she felt like a solid couple with him.

He half heard the bus driver telling the tourists that the Catalina Mansion was the only mansion ever built on the island.

He tried to figure out the right words that wouldn't hurt her. But the sweet smell of her hair was paradise. Her laughter was like a melody to his ears. He couldn't stop looking at her, oblivious to the world around him.

"You're missing the great view," she said, motioning to the vast blue Pacific Ocean.

"I've got the best view of all," he said, knowing no woman could ever match her, not ever.

A few minutes later the bus came to a stop, and the driver called out, "In two hours, I'll sound the bus horn for all of you to meet back here."

During the tour of the majestic mansion, he kept thinking about how he'd bring up the marriage topic. But she kept oohhing and ahhing about the elegant furnishings in each room.

"Garrett, this mansion is exquisite," she said. "But I'd like a cozy house for my family someday." She looked up at him. "What about you?"

I could live anywhere as long as I'm with you, he wanted to tell her. Instead, he said, "A small place is perfect for me, too."

The tour began heading into the last room. But Elena grabbed his hand and led him out to the balcony instead, overlooking the trees, houses and harbor of Catalina Island.

She slipped her arm through his and leaned her head against his shoulder. "Garrett, I love being here with you," she said.

His heart swelled. He lifted her chin with his finger and gazed at her as the ocean breeze blew back her satin hair. He drew her into his arms and held her close to his body, never wanting to let her go.

Before he knew it, the words flowed from his lips, "Elena, I wish I could stay on Catalina Island with you forever."

"Garrett, I do, too!"

Then she kissed him with a fervor he'd never felt from her before. A warm kiss that spoke of how much she cared. An emotional kiss that silently told him that she wanted to be a permanent part of his life.

As his tongue blended with hers, the blaring bus horn cut into their kiss, alerting him that he'd gotten so caught up in his feelings for her that he hadn't told her about his inner doubts.

As the bus drove down the hillside to the City of Avalon, Garrett stared out the window, not knowing how to reveal to her the dark shadows in his heart.

"Garrett, is something wrong?" she asked as the bus parked, and she followed him out.

"Everything's perfect," he replied, dreading to say the words that would ruin the special feeling he had with her.

She stopped in front of a quaint souvenir shop. "Do you mind if I go in and pick out souvenirs for my nephews and sister?"

"Let's do it," he said, following her inside.

She slipped her arm through his and went into the store. As she checked out gifts for her family, he glanced at the one-hundred-piece puzzle of Catalina Island on the shelf. He felt like his turmoiled thoughts were in a hundred different fragments, just like the puzzle.

After several minutes choosing souvenirs, Elena stood at the cashier with replica sea dollars and starfish from Catalina Island's marine life for her nephews and a sea-shell bracelet for Jan.

She glanced worriedly at Garrett who was waiting for her outside the store. He was staring at the harbor where a bunch of dark clouds loomed in the distance, threatening rain.

Ever since she'd gotten on the charter boat with him, she'd sensed that he was troubled about something. She was sure he was still bothered by the deal she'd gotten for Stanley. No matter how close she wanted to be with him, the reality of her being ahead of him for the vice president job still threatened their relationship.

She picked up the paid bag of souvenirs and tried not to think about the promotion. If she wanted their last Marriage Connection date to go perfectly, she had to focus on enjoying every second with the man she cared about—the man she hoped to be with forever.

As she walked out of the store, she immediately noticed the crease line of worry on Garrett's forehead. She had to get his mind off their career conflict and back on just the two of them.

She walked up behind him and slipped her arms around his waist, resting her cheek against his broad back, feeling the solidness of him. He warmly covered her hands with his palms.

"Finished shopping?" he asked.

"Umm-hmm. Why don't we have lunch?"

"You read my mind," he said, turning around and holding her close. "I saw a great restaurant down the street."

"Excellent," she said. "Afterward, maybe we can take a walk in the mountains."

"I bought us a trail map in the souvenir shop."

"We're in sync!" she said, knowing he was so perfect for her.

After lunch, as Elena walked up a mountain trail through lush green trees with Garrett, she still sensed that he was troubled, and she didn't know what to do.

"Elena, watch out for the poison oak!" he called out, protectively grabbing her hand and pulling her near him, away from the poison green leaves growing alongside the trail.

As she felt his protective arm around her, she yearned to hear him say that their third date wouldn't be their last one. She wanted to hear him say that he'd always be with her.

He picked a tiny perfumed purple flower, and as she smelled the sweet scent, he looked at her, as though he wanted to tell her something. From the worried expression in his eyes, she was afraid he was going to bring up their competitive job situation. She couldn't let their work conflict prevent her dream of a future with him.

"Look, Garrett!" she quickly said, pointing up ahead. "There's a brook!"

She ran toward the bubbling water, reaching the round stones that would take her across the water to the other side. She pulled off her shoes and set her feet on the slippery stones. The cool mountain water sprinkled over her feet.

As she glanced back to see where Garrett was, her foot suddenly slipped off the rock. Her knee twisted, and she fell into the cold brook water.

In the next instant she felt Garrett lifting her into his arms and setting her down on the dry grass.

"Are you hurt?" he asked in a worried voice.

"I may have sprained my knee a little," she replied, feeling a hint of strain over her right kneecap. "I'm so clumsy. First, the ballpark. Now Catalina Island. I'm such a burden to you."

"No, you're not," he said, his gaze holding hers. "I like taking care of you, Elena."

"You do?" she asked, waiting to hear the magic words that would create a life for them together.

Instead, she saw a streak of lightning course through the mountain area followed by a crack of thunder. Huge raindrops began to fall.

She was about to stand up, but Garrett grabbed her souvenir bag and lifted her into his arms.

"I don't want to take any chances with your knee," he said.

As the rain poured down on them, she held Garrett around the neck while he carried her down the trail, feeling safe and secure in his arms.

She looked up at his handsome face as he climbed down the muddy trail. She stared at his chiseled features as the raindrops wet his face. Her eyes lingered on the sensual shape of his mouth. Her body stirred as she thought about his mouth on her naked skin.

His eyes met hers, as though he could read her fantasy.

"Garrett, if I'm getting too heavy, I could walk," she

forced out, conscious of his hard, muscled body against hers.

"I can handle you just fine, Elena," he said, tightening his grip on her.

Feeling a rush of warm love for him, she wiped the raindrops off his cheeks and then his lips, feeling like he was her man, wanting to whisper loving words to him that she'd never said to any man before.

The rain poured down as Garrett reached the bottom of the mountain trail with Elena in his arms. Lightning streaked across the sky, and a strong wind blew at his back.

He barely noticed. He was more conscious of the feel of Elena's gentle fingers wiping the raindrops from his face. Her caress sent a radiating heat through his body.

As he reached Avalon, with her soaked body against his, he noticed that her midriff top clung skintight to her breasts. He could see the outline of her bra and the peak of her nipples.

He swallowed, forcing his gaze away, looking for dry shelter.

"Garrett, I think I can walk okay," she said.

"Are you sure?"

She nodded, and he put her down to her feet, missing the feel of her soft body close to his.

She glanced at her watch. "Garrett, it's four o'clock!" she quickly said. "The charter boat should be leaving for San Pedro Harbor any minute now!"

"Come on," he said, grabbing her hand.

He felt anxious as they headed for the boat office. He still hadn't shared his doubts with her. He didn't know how to say it, without destroying the incredible closeness he felt with her.

Inside the boat office he found a crowd of passengers

flocking near the desk. The captain of the charter boat waved for everyone's attention.

"I'm terribly sorry, folks," he began. "The trip back to San Pedro has been canceled. We can't risk traveling at sea with that lightning and wind."

"When's the next boat?" Garrett called out.

"Eight tomorrow morning," the man replied.

Garrett glanced at Elena, realizing he'd have to stay overnight on the island with her, immediately fantasizing about sharing the same bed with her.

"Garrett, we'd better get hotel rooms," she said.

Two rooms, not one, he reminded himself.

He turned to the office clerk. "Can you steer us to the nearest hotel?"

"With all these passengers looking for rooms?" the woman said, shaking her head. "You'll be lucky if you find a vacant spot."

The woman handed him a list of hotels and pointed to the public phones where people were hurrying to make reservations.

He squeezed Elena's hand. "I'll find us a bed," he said, immediately realizing that he sounded as if he were talking about one bed for the two of them to make love in.

Before he could explain himself, he saw a phone open. While Elena waited, he hurried over and started calling. After talking to almost every hotel and bed-and-breakfast place near the harbor, he discovered that every room was booked up. He quickly dialed the last hotel on the island, which was a distance from the harbor and asked if there were two vacant rooms.

The woman on the phone didn't speak English very well, but he heard her say that she definitely had space.

He left his name and hung up. "We've got rooms," he told Elena, putting his arm around her shivering wet body to give her warmth.

"Great," she said, leaning close to him. "I knew you'd take care of us."

Us. He wanted the word to mean the two of them for eternity, but something deep inside made him feel the idea could never come true for him.

The rain was coming down in sheets as he hurried out with her to a car service which drove them to a funky-looking hotel in need of a paint job.

As he entered the lobby with Elena, he noticed that the furniture was clean but very worn.

"Elena, I never thought the place would look like this," he said apologetically.

"As long as we have rooms for the night," she said. "That's what matters."

As she excused herself to go to the lobby rest room, Garrett walked up to the elderly woman at the registration desk and gave his name.

"Yes, yes, I remember you called," she said with a thick accent. "Here is the key to room nineteen. The sheets are fresh. The towels are in the bathroom."

"I also need the key to the other room," he said.

"Other room?" she repeated, confused. "There is only one room left."

Garrett anxiously glanced toward the closed rest room door, wanting to stay in one room with her, yet knowing he couldn't, not when he hadn't told her the truth about his hesitancy to get married again.

In the hotel rest room, Elena brushed her wet hair. She was so nervous being at a hotel with Garrett that she could hardly think straight. A feeling of exhilaration rushed through her at the thought of remaining with him longer, knowing their last date wasn't over yet.

As she opened the door of the rest room, she saw Gar-

rett at the registration desk getting their rooms. His wet
T-shirt and shorts were molded to his muscled body.

"Garrett, did you get the room keys?" she asked as
she approached him.

"We've got kind of a problem," he hesitantly began.
"There's only one room."

"One room?" she repeated, her fantasies about making
love to him going on overwhelm.

"You can have the room," he quickly said. "I'll call
other hotels again. Maybe someone's canceled out."

"Garrett, the island's full," she said. "We've got no
other choice."

"Only if you feel okay about it."

"I'm fine," she said, aching to be alone with him, yet
knowing she needed to hold back the desire to give all of
herself to him.

The moment Garrett unlocked the hotel room door,
Elena's gaze landed on the bed. One bed. Double size.
Just for him and her.

She immediately pictured him naked under the sheets
with her. She pushed the thought aside, knowing she
couldn't get that vulnerable with him until she was completely sure that he wanted a life with her.

"You're trembling," he said, touching her shoulders.

"My body feels so cold."

"I'll get a warm bath started for you," he said, heading
for the bathroom.

"I'll call my sister to tell her that the boat's been de-
layed."

She nervously dialed Jan's number, conscious of Garrett being just a few feet away from her in the bathroom.

"Jan," she began, trying to keep her voice steady.
"The boat's been rescheduled for tomorrow morning because of a thunderstorm."

"Where are you staying for the night?" her sister asked, concerned.

"In a hotel room."

"With Garrett?"

"There was only one room left and—"

"Where's Garrett now?"

She could hear him running water in the tub. "He's preparing a bath," she responded.

"For the two of you?" her sister asked excitedly.

"Just for me," she quickly replied. "I caught a chill from walking in the rain."

"El, don't doubt his feelings for you," Jan told her. "Can't you see how much he cares?"

"Oh, Jan," she whispered. "I almost feel like he's my—" She stopped, hearing the bath water turn off. "I've got to go. See you tomorrow morning."

She hung up the phone just as Garrett walked into the bedroom. He tenderly wrapped a dry bath towel around her wet shoulders. "The bath's all set."

"You're wonderful," she said, unable to stop herself. "I'll hurry so you can take one, too."

As she went into the bathroom to shed her wet clothes, she felt a momentary tinge of pain in her knee. But she was too excited and nervous to care. She closed the bathroom door, feeling the crazy impulse to ask Garrett in, but she didn't dare follow her desire.

Garrett anxiously turned on the hotel television set, flipping the channels, going nowhere. All he could think about was Elena slipping off her wet clothes in the bathroom and standing naked on the other side of the thin wooden door.

He snapped off the set, feeling frustrated with himself. He still hadn't shared his doubts about marriage with her. Every time he thought of bringing it up, the words wouldn't come out. He knew he was putting it off. He wanted to be close to her for just a little while longer.

Just then, he heard a groan coming from the bathroom. He went to the closed door. "Elena, are you all right?"

"My knee buckled as I was about to get into the tub," she said in a worried voice.

Without thinking, Garrett barreled into the bathroom. He saw her sitting on the outside edge of the bathtub— naked—rubbing her knee.

"I'll help you into the tub," he offered, gently grabbing her by the waist.

"My knee hurt for just an instant," she said, "but I think it'll be okay."

"The warm water will soothe it," he told her, trying to keep his voice steady.

As he helped her into the tub, he realized that his hands grazed her swollen breasts. His gaze drifted to her feminine patch peeking out at him from under the water.

A hot desire rose up within him, and when he looked up, she was staring at him with longing in her eyes, a vulnerability that he couldn't resist.

His heart pounded. All rational thinking left his mind. When he leaned over and kissed her parted lips, she spread her fingers through his hair, drawing him closer to her.

He slipped his hands under the warm water and cupped her bare breasts. As he squeezed her firm mounds, her nipples rose to his touch.

He glided his hand down her abdomen and across her velvet inner thighs. She moaned as he caressed her femininity under the bath water. A jolt of arousal radiated through his being as he felt her spasm at his touch.

Suddenly the porcelain of the bathtub became an obstacle between his body and hers. He felt her hands lift up his wet T-shirt, and he quickly discarded his clothes on the bathroom floor.

As he climbed into the warm water, he forgot about all of his doubts. All he was aware of was his need to get as close as he could to the woman who mattered the most to him.

As he sat in the tub, he lifted her onto his lap to face him. He hungrily blended his mouth with hers, nibbling, biting. When he felt her hand grasp his masculinity, he groaned from the intense sensations of her caress.

"Elena, I want you," he murmured, needing to fuse his body and soul with hers.

"I want you, too," she whispered back.

She fondled his masculinity until he felt explosive, and he slipped his manhood inside of her.

"Oh, Garrett," she groaned, raising both hands to his head, grasping his hair as he moved in and out of her.

"You feel so good to me, Elena, so good."

He lifted her slightly and cupped her firm buttocks in both hands, plunging deeper, feeling as though his spirit was touching hers, as though their life force was becoming one.

She arched her back, drawing him even deeper inside of her. He covered her breasts with his mouth, licking, tasting, nibbling. He wanted all of her, and he needed to give all of himself.

In the midst of his passion and closeness to her, he heard himself whisper the words he thought he'd never reveal. "I love you so much, Elena," he whispered. "I'll always love you."

"Oh, Garrett, I love you, too!" she said back, rhythmically moving in total unison with him.

He grasped her tighter to him, needing to get even closer, feeling a crescendo of emotion building to an explosive peak. Her body began to tremble and spasm, and then he could no longer hold back. His juices burst deep inside of her.

Afterward, as he tenderly held her in his arms, love for her poured from his heart like an unending stream.

"Elena, I never thought I could feel this close to anyone," he whispered.

"I love being close to you, Garrett," she whispered back.

She took his hand and got out of the tub with him. Then she began drying off his naked body with a towel. As she sensually stroked his thighs with the terry cloth, his libido responded.

"I want you again, Elena," he groaned, lifting her in his arms and carrying her to the bed. He gazed at her naked beauty lying on the bedspread. He realized that he'd never get enough of her.

She tenderly grabbed him around the neck and pulled him down on top of her. Within seconds he was inside of her again, renewing their passion, rejuvenated by the love they shared.

Later, wrapped in a blanket of bliss, Garrett fell asleep in Elena's arms, totally content, completely fulfilled being with the woman he loved.

The rising orange sun through the hotel window barely woke him up. He felt like he was in an incredible dream with Elena. His cheek was against her naked breast. Feeling a stirring of arousal, he put his lips to her brown nipple.

She moaned as his tongue circled her breast, nibbling her firm flesh. His mouth traveled down her belly, tasting the sweet honey of her skin.

As he moved farther down her body under the sheet, she spread her legs in response. His lips touched the hot flesh of her inner thighs and slid up to her femininity.

"Garrett, oh, Garrett," she whispered with such love in her voice that he felt like he was the universe to her.

As he felt her spasm against his mouth, his manhood responded to her arousal. Her fingers gripped his hair, and he met her lips with his as he slipped his masculinity deep inside her.

He groaned as electrical sensations flooded through his body. He felt complete, so complete, being inside of her. She was everything to him. Nothing else existed except Elena.

As the peak of passion tensed up his body, he tried to hold back, wanting to share the intense pleasure with her for a few moments longer. Then he felt a tremor of uncontrollable ecstasy, and he surrendered to the explosion of becoming one with her.

As he held her naked body against him in the glow of love, she whispered against his lips, "Garrett, we better hurry or we'll miss the boat."

"The boat?" he repeated, oblivious to everything except being with her.

She slipped free. "Come on!" she said, smiling, her eyes glimmering with happiness. "Or we'll have to swim home!"

As she got out of bed, the reality of his making love to her hit him like a steel beam across the chest.

"Garrett, I've never felt so happy in my entire life!" she said as she hurried to take a shower.

He abruptly sat up in bed, suddenly unable to breathe. He'd just shared the ultimate intimate experience with her. He felt a contentment with her that he'd never known before.

Yet an intensely anxious feeling rose up in him that he could barely control. He realized that Elena had completely entered his heart. She meant everything to him. But he knew how love could end up in his life.

*   *   *

On the outer deck of the crowded charter boat with Elena, Garrett's eyes were trained on a young couple hugging nearby. The rays of the morning sun sparkled off the man's gold wedding band. Just like a ring he once wore. A ring he thought he'd never take off.

As Elena leaned against his shoulder, he felt a deep love for her that overwhelmed him. But doubts about her staying with him for always kept rising up in his mind.

As the boat docked at San Pedro Harbor, the crowd started to rush off the boat. He was momentarily separated from Elena as an employee on the ship motioned him aside to sign the last dating service release form.

He scribbled his name. When he looked for her, she was way ahead in the crowd, waving for him to follow her as she hurried toward her family, waiting in a parked station wagon in the distance.

He stopped walking, knowing he couldn't meet her sister. He had no right to be a part of her wonderful family. He'd gotten so immersed in her on Catalina Island, so totally caught up in his intense feelings for her, that he hadn't shared that part of him which troubled him the most.

"Elena!" he called out before she reached the station wagon. When she turned around, he said, "I've got to get home. I'll call you!"

"Okay!" she called back, her eyes glowing with warmth for him.

As Garrett drove out of the parking lot, his emotions were more fragmented than ever.

Nine

In the station wagon, as her sister drove, Elena leaned back in the front seat, feeling ecstatic about her love night with Garrett.

"Why didn't I get to meet your man?" Jan asked.

My man. She loved the sound of those words. "You will, another time," she replied.

She wanted very much for her sister to know the man she loved. But she knew it wasn't the right time, not until the promotion was settled, and their minds were clear to love.

Her sister glanced at her. "Don't keep me waiting a second longer," she said in a low voice so the kids didn't hear. "What happened last night?"

A feeling of incredible happiness spread over her just thinking about her and Garrett naked in the tub and on the bed together.

"He made love to me all night long," she whispered, trying to contain her excitement.

"I knew it!" Jan said, watching the road ahead of her. "The moment you got in the car I could tell."

"You could?" she said. "Jan, he told me that he loved me!"

"Oh, El, I'm so happy for you!" her sister gushed. "What else did he say?"

She knew Jan wanted to hear the words he'd said about their future together. Words he hadn't expressed yet.

"He loves me, Jan," she replied, not caring about anything else. "That's all that matters."

As she entered her apartment, she couldn't help fantasizing about his proposing to her. But she knew she had to wait.

She lay down on her bed, wishing the promotion decision was already made. As she fell asleep, she dreamed that she was Garrett's wife.

The next few days at work felt torturous as she waited for Stanley's decision. Then, one morning, Stanley waved her into his office as he was talking on the phone.

Her stomach was in knots as she sat down while he finished his phone call. "If she's not doing a good job at my company," she overheard him say, "then maybe we need to let her go." Then he hung up.

"Elena, if you have any further innovative business deals, let me know right away," he said. "Garrett called me. He's moved up with new accounts. I plan to make my decision this week."

"Sure thing," she said, feeling in a sudden panic at his words.

Returning to her desk, she wondered how many new accounts Garrett had gotten. She'd been almost ninety percent sure that she would get the vice president paycheck that would solve her financial problems. Now she wasn't so sure anymore.

She grabbed her bag and headed out to a real estate

office in Pacific Palisades that had just opened, hoping she could find more new accounts. As she drove through the Palisades, she worried about how the promotion was going to affect the love between her and Garrett.

If she got the job, wouldn't he resent her, even if he tried to hide it from himself? And if he got the promotion, she knew he'd feel guilty that he'd hurt her in the process.

She couldn't risk losing him because of a job!

She felt torn inside as she entered the Realtor's office. There were a couple of business people talking to real estate agents. As she introduced herself, she kept worrying about her relationship with Garrett.

"Elena Martin?" a graying gentleman in his late forties began with an extended hand. "I'm Peter Drexler, president of Drexler Property Management."

"Hello," she said, shaking his hand, aware that his company was a major competitor of Stanley's in the property management field.

"I heard about the profitable business merger you arranged for Stanley Grant," the businessman went on. "I must admit, every management-firm owner in Los Angeles envied him on that one."

She smiled. "Thank you. I think Stanley is very pleased."

"He is quite fortunate having a savvy manager like you working for him," Drexler continued. "I could certainly use your skill and talent at my company. Would you ever consider leaving Grant Property Management for a more lucrative job?"

Elena was taken aback. A few weeks ago she would never have considered leaving her job with Stanley. But Garrett flashed into her head.

"Exactly what do you have in mind?" she heard herself inquire.

Her mind raced as Peter Drexler proposed a benefits

package and annual salary that would equal the raise she'd get if she became vice president with Stanley. An increase that would more than satisfy her need to financially help out her sister. *And* she could still have her relationship with Garrett!

"Do we have a deal, Ms. Martin?" the businessman asked.

Not wanting to leave Grant Property Management, but knowing she had to, she took a deep breath and said, "We definitely have a deal."

As she shook Peter Drexler's hand to confirm the arrangement, she felt bittersweet about her decision, knowing she was giving up the status job she'd dreamed of getting, but knowing she'd be keeping Garrett in her life for always.

As Garrett anxiously waited for wealthy financier, Morgan Streit, to get off the phone so he could discuss his ideas for property management, he desperately searched for the right words to tell Elena that marriage wasn't for him.

Words that wouldn't hurt her. Words that might still keep her in his life.

He knew he was thinking the impossible. Why would she stay with him if she thought that marriage wasn't a possibility?

Yet he loved her more than he ever dreamed he could care about a woman. And the intensity of his emotions made him feel totally off balance.

"Mr. Sims, what exactly do you propose?"

"Marriage," Garrett blurted, suddenly realizing that the tycoon was off the phone.

He hoped he hadn't blown it, with his mind so absorbed by Elena. Morgan Streit had five commercial buildings under construction in Los Angeles County. There was a lot of money involved. With the three other accounts he'd recently gotten, a more-than-lucrative contract with Streit would completely equal the profit of Elena's new accounts.

"Mr. Streit, I promise to give you great management that will keep your profits high, your expenses low and provide superb service to your business tenants."

"Show me figures, Mr. Sims."

"Right here," Garrett said.

As he laid out his detailed budget sheets, he wondered if he should call Elena and tell her that he needed to talk. But what would he say? Should he bluntly tell her that marriage didn't work for him?

He knew he couldn't say that to her. Because the real question gnawing at his insides, the one he knew he could never ask her was, *Will you ever leave me?*

Morgan Streit reviewed the financial plan and closed the folder. "Your budget strategy is economical and sound," the financier said. "Let's get the papers rolling."

In his car Garrett dialed Stanley's number on the cell phone to tell him. As the phone rang, he was relieved that his new accounts equaled but didn't surpass Elena's and that Stanley's decision would have to be a fair one.

When he got Grace on the phone, she told him that Stanley went home early because he wasn't feeling well. Garrett hesitated, wanting to ask to speak to Elena, but he knew he couldn't share his doubts over the phone, not after the intimacy he'd shared with her. He had to tell her in person. But how?

Filled with turmoil, he called Trey. "Can you meet me at the pool hall tonight?" he asked his friend over the line.

"I'm married, remember?" his buddy replied. "Come over for dinner. I'm cooking Chinese."

When Garrett arrived at Trey's, he was all set to talk

about his confused feelings about marriage and Elena
when he noticed that Julie was angry with Trey. He realized that his friend had neglected to tell his wife that he
was coming.

At the dinner table, Garrett shifted uncomfortably in his
seat as Julie argued with Trey about how inconsiderate he
was and how he hadn't changed at all.

Before Garrett even tasted the sweet and sour chicken,
Julie stormed out of the kitchen.

"Trey, maybe I better go," Garrett began.

"Stay and eat," his friend said. "I'll be right back."
Then he went to his wife.

He couldn't eat a thing on his plate. He felt more confused than ever about his feelings about getting married
again. If he gave his heart and soul to Elena in marriage,
he could never handle it if she ever left him.

A few minutes later, Trey returned with his arm around
Julie. She looked at bit embarrassed.

"Garrett, after seeing us together," she began, "you
probably never want to walk down the aisle again."

Before he could answer, Trey said, "Don't worry about
that, Julie. Garrett's too scared to get married again."

"I am not," he said defensively.

"Sure you are," his friend pushed. "You're waiting
for a new clause to be put in the marriage contract."

"What clause?"

"The one that states, This marriage is guaranteed to
work."

Later, in his apartment, Garrett couldn't sleep. His
friend's words played in his mind. He did want a guarantee that marriage would last for him. Because no matter
how hard he tried, he couldn't convince himself that Elena
would definitely stay with him for the rest of her life.

As Elena hurried into the Santa Monica office, she felt
unsure about giving her notice to Stanley. She had to re-

mind herself that she was quitting her job for her and Garrett. Then he'd be free to get the V.P. position, and she could share her life with him forever.

Just as she was mentally practicing the best approach to tell Stanley, her boss walked into her cubicle. He had dark shadows under his eyes and a concerned look on his face. She immediately felt uneasy.

"Elena, can I have a word with you?" he said in a strained voice. Then he walked back into his office without waiting for her reply.

She nervously bit her bottom lip. Had Stanley somehow found out about her new job before she'd gotten to him first? She hoped not. Stanley had been good to her. She'd never want him to think she was being disloyal when he'd given her so much encouragement at the company.

As she headed toward Stanley's office, she glanced at Grace, hoping she could get a clue from her. But the receptionist was busy answering telephones.

She took a deep breath and entered her boss's office. She stopped dead in her tracks when she saw Garrett standing inside. His distressed eyes silently told her there was trouble, big trouble.

Stanley motioned for Elena to sit in the chair across from his desk. "This is very awkward for me, Elena."

"Please, Stan," Garrett cut in. "Don't bring Elena into this. I'm completely responsible."

"I've got no other choice, Garrett," he finally said. "Elena, on Monday, I fired Delia, the secretary at my Sherman Oaks branch. To retaliate she told me that you and Garrett are romantically involved."

"I—" her voice caught as her eyes darted to Garrett. She flashed on Delia catching them in a moment of passion at his office. A moment of love that was going to destroy everything.

"Elena, I have no right to pry into anyone's private life," Stanley continued. "However, the last romantic relationship in my office drastically affected my business. I can't have that happen again."

"I told you, Stan," Garrett pushed. "The entire thing is my fault."

"No, Garrett," she said, knowing he couldn't take the blame.

He looked at her with pleading eyes. She knew he was trying to protect her, and she loved him even more.

Stanley stood up. He looked pale and almost unsteady on his feet. "If the accusation is true," he went on, "I leave it to the two of you to work it out."

Panicking, she had to do something! She didn't want Garrett to lose his chance at becoming vice president because of her. She had to immediately give her notice to quit the job.

"Stanley," she began, "I need to tell you that I—"

Before she could continue, Stanley gripped the side of the desk. His face creased in pain. She hurried over to him as Garrett helped him back down onto the chair.

She quickly picked up the phone. "I'll call the paramedics."

"No," Stanley forced out. "I can't wait that long. Garrett, can you take me to the hospital?"

"We're on the way, Stan," he said reassuringly.

She helped get Stanley down to the parking lot and into Garrett's Mustang. As she was about to get into the back seat, her boss said, "Elena, I've got a lot of phone messages on my desk. Can you handle the calls for me?"

"Sure, Stanley," she said. "I'll take care of it. You just get well."

She caught Garrett's eye, wishing she could tell him that she loved him and that she hoped what happened with Stanley and their jobs wouldn't hurt their relationship.

When she got back to the office, Grace asked worriedly, "Is Stanley going to be okay?"

"I hope so," she replied.

"Elena, don't be mad at me for saying this," Grace hesitantly began. "Everyone in the office knows what Delia said."

She could feel the blood rushing up to her face. "I really messed up, Grace."

"No, you didn't," the woman told her. "I think you and Garrett make a great couple."

She filled with emotion. "Thanks, Grace, thanks so much," she said, giving her a warm hug.

Then she hurried into Stanley's office to deal with his messages. She tried to focus on talking to clients on the phone, but all she could think about was Garrett. What if he didn't get the vice presidency job because of their office romance? Would he blame her?

Stanley's intercom buzzed. "Elena," Grace began, "the new receptionist at the Sherman Oaks office just called. Garrett got a phone message from an upset tenant at the property he manages in Palms. Should we give the tenant his cellular phone number?"

"No, don't bother him at the hospital," she told her. "I'll handle the problem for him."

She called the tenant, wanting to help Garrett. The tenant was in a panic.

"A bunch of water pipes burst in our building!" the woman told her. "Water is dripping from the ceiling!"

"Give me the address of your building," she told her, quickly noting the building number. "I'll get right on it." Then she buzzed Grace. "Get me the plumbing vendor that Garrett uses. Hurry!"

The moment she got the plumber on the line, she instructed him to immediately call the tenant to tell her how to shut off the building's water system. Then she told him to rush over to the apartment building, and she'd meet him there.

She grabbed her bag and momentarily stopped at Grace's desk. "Call Garrett at the hospital," she told Grace, handing her a sheet of paper. "Tell him that I'm handling a building problem for him at this Palms address."

"I'll call him pronto," Grace replied.

"Grace, get hold of the owner, too," she added. "I need to get a list of the tenants and a set of keys to all the apartments."

Grace started dialing. "I'll call the owner right away so you'll have the keys waiting for you when you get there."

As Elena drove to the complex, her thoughts were on how she wanted Garrett to know that she'd always be there for him, whether in business or love.

She ached to call him to find out not only how Stanley was, but if his feelings for her had changed.

At the building in Palms, she met the plumbing vendor who'd recently repaired the water pipes.

"Ms. Martin, I am sorry about the leak problem," he said. "I'll have all damage to the apartments repaired." He told her that the owner had dropped off the tenant list and a set of apartment keys, which he handed to her.

She briefly glanced at the tenant list and noticed that next to each tenant's name was the date they moved in.

She started knocking on every apartment door to check for water damage, wanting to do a perfect job for Garrett, wanting him to know that he could always depend on her. She was determined to do everything in her power to keep their love safe and secure. But she couldn't stop worrying that he could lose the job he'd worked so hard to get—because of her.

A couple of tenants were home, and she and the

plumber went inside. The apartment doors that weren't answered, she unlocked with the key and checked off the tenant's name so that she could let them know that she'd been in their place.

As she continued her apartment inspections, she stopped at apartment twenty-eight and turned to the plumber. "How many families live in this complex?" she asked, not having time to count how many apartments were left and needing to hurry and finish the work. She needed to get to the hospital to see Garrett and find out about Stanley.

"Ms. Martin, there are no families in this building," the plumber replied. "This is a singles-only complex."

"No marrieds?" she said, ringing the doorbell of apartment twenty-eight. She thought about her and Garrett renting a cute apartment, just the two of them. She hoped her dream could still come true.

"Definitely no married couples," the man replied. "Every tenant who lives here signs a lease agreeing to live a single's life for the next two years." The plumber walked to the next apartment. "I'll check for leaks next door."

As she knocked on the door of twenty-eight, she couldn't imagine living in a singles-only place, not when she wanted to be married to Garrett.

"I'm here from Grant Property Management," she called through the door. "I'd like to come inside to see if you have any leaks."

After receiving no response, she slipped the key into the lock. "I'm coming inside," she said.

When she opened the door, the apartment felt oddly familiar to her. The black leather sofa. The teak coffee table with magazines strewn on top. And the musk scent in the air.

Suddenly her breath caught. She spotted a geometric-patterned tie lying on the sofa. A feeling of dread washed over her. Her hands started to tremble as she flipped through the list of apartment numbers and came to apartment twenty-eight.

Her heartbeat stopped as she stared at the name "Garrett Sims" as the tenant. Her eyes froze on the date he'd moved in, agreeing to live a singles life for the next two years.

Her body felt numb. He'd moved in while he was dating her. When he was telling her that he loved her. While she was waiting for him to ask her to marry him.

In the hospital waiting room, Garrett gripped his cell phone so tight that his knuckles turned white. All he could hear was Grace telling him that Elena was handling the broken pipe problem at the apartment building in Palms that he managed. The singles-only apartment complex that he lived in! He didn't remember hanging up.

He barely heard the male nurse walk into the waiting room. "Mr. Sims, the doctor is giving Mr. Grant some tests."

"Is he going to be all right?" he asked worriedly.

"I think so," the man replied. "We'll call you into the room shortly."

"Yes, thanks, thanks a lot," he pushed out, his mind in a major panic.

Garrett started pacing the waiting room floor, nervously running his fingers through his hair. He was angry at himself for putting off telling her the truth about his need to remain single. He had wanted to hold onto the close feeling with her a little while longer. And now his need might explode in his face.

He wanted to immediately rush to the apartment complex to talk to her. But he couldn't leave Stanley. He flipped open his phone, anxiously dialing Elena's cell phone number, needing to talk to her, needing to explain.

Before he could do so, the nurse returned to the waiting room. "Mr. Sims, you can come into the room now."

He snapped closed the phone and hurried to the hospital room where he found Stanley lying in bed.

"Stan, how are you feeling?" he asked, trying to contain his high level of anxiety about Elena.

"I'm still kicking," he said, attempting a smile. "The doctor said I had a very mild heart attack. She says if I don't slow down, the next time I won't be so lucky."

"You better listen to her advice, Stan," he told him, concerned.

"I will," he said. "It looks like I'll need to retire earlier than scheduled." He stopped, as though he were trying to digest the new turn in his life. "Garrett, I'm giving you the job."

"What about Elena?" he couldn't help but ask. "She's worked as hard, if not harder, than I have to get the promotion."

He couldn't believe what he was saying. Stanley was handing him the job he badly wanted and now he was pushing for Elena!

"She's an excellent manager," Stanley agreed. "But you've been with me longer, Garrett. I trust you. And if the position works out for you, I want you to run my entire company."

The nurse came in, bringing a medication tray. As he was instructing Stanley that he needed to remain overnight for observation, Garrett stared out the window, feeling like his insides were being severed in half.

He wanted to feel elated that his career dream was happening. He wanted to let Stanley know how grateful he was for the promotion and the words of promise for his business future. Yet he felt a deep anguish, knowing how crushed Elena would be when she learned that she wouldn't get the job.

"Garrett, you haven't given a yes or no to my offer," Stanley said when the nurse left.

"Stan, I'm honored you chose me," he began. "But we've still got the problem of my relationship with Elena."

"You know how I feel about that situation, Garrett."

"Yes, I do," he said. "But I can only accept the promotion under two circumstances."

"What's that, Garrett?"

"If I'm vice president," he went on, "it must be with the understanding that Elena remains at the company."

Stanley was silent for a long moment, and Garrett's body tightened, wondering how far he'd pushed him. He knew he was risking his entire future with the company for Elena, but he couldn't allow her to lose her job because of him.

"Garrett, what is condition number two?" Stanley asked.

He took a deep breath of oxygen. "As vice president, I want to give Elena a substantial pay increase for her incredible work at the company." He knew she deserved it. He knew she needed that money to help out her sister and nephews.

"I see," his boss pondered. "You're asking a lot of me, Garrett."

"I realize that, Stan," he said, hoping he hadn't thrown away his entire career at the company. "But I'd never do anything to adversely affect the success of your business."

Stanley took a long sip of water. "I know I must totally trust your judgment if I'm to eventually let you head my entire company." He held out his hand. "Your two conditions are accepted in full."

Garrett firmly shook his hand. "Thank you, Stan. You won't regret it."

The nurse peaked his head in. "Mr. Grant, you need to rest now."

"Stan, I'll be back tomorrow morning to take you home," he said as he left the room.

In his car Garrett struggled to maintain the speed limit as he raced to his apartment building in Palms to see Elena. How was he going to tell her that he got the promotion and not her? How would he reveal to her that though he was powerful and successful in business, he was a man who'd failed at love before, and in that area of life, he had no confidence at all.

As he made a sharp stop in front of the singles-only apartment building, he phoned Grace at the office to inform her that Stanley would be fine and also let her know that he was at the apartment complex.

He hurried into the lobby, searching for the plumbing vendor, knowing Elena would probably be with him making sure the pipe problem was solved.

He searched every apartment on the first floor, but she wasn't there. He flew up the staircase two steps at a time to the second floor, where his apartment was located.

His blood was pumping full speed through his veins. His breathing was out of control. At the far end of the hall, way past his apartment, he noticed an open door. His muscles tensed as he walked toward it and saw Elena in the living room, heading for the kitchen, jotting notes onto a pad.

Before he could speak, he heard the plumber call out from down the hall, "Garrett, I'm very sorry for the mess-up!"

He saw Elena's hand freeze on the page. Her face turned pale. He knew she was aware of him at the doorway, but she didn't look up, acting as though he didn't exist. She walked into the kitchen and bent down to open the cabinet door under the sink.

The plumber was at his side. He could barely hear him talking. "Garrett, I'm repairing the pipes right now," he said. "Elena has done a terrific job alerting all the tenants. She's checked every single apartment on both floors, except the one next door."

He couldn't breathe. *She's already been to my place!* He watched her walk toward the door where he was standing.

"There's some water dripping under the kitchen sink," she said to the plumber, totally ignoring him.

"I'll take care of it," the man said.

"I'll check next door," she told the plumber, her eyes deliberately not meeting his.

Then she walked past him, as though he was invisible, with her heart as cold as Antarctica.

He stood there, feeling the steel wall between them— the wall he'd caused by not being totally open about his feelings with her.

Unable to give up, he followed her into the apartment next door, hoping, praying, she'd listen to him.

Ten

In the tenant's apartment, Elena struggled to hold back her torrential feelings as she blindly checked the bathroom for leaks. She suddenly felt Garrett behind her. She didn't dare look at him. She didn't want him to see the pain radiating from her heart.

"Elena, I want to explain—" he began.

She angrily whirled around. "Explain what?" she fired back. "That you pretended to love me? That you pretended to want a future relationship with me by signing the Marriage Connection agreement? You're a liar, Garrett Sims. All along you planned to remain single!"

Swallowing back a sob, she rushed out of the apartment.

"Elena!" he called out.

She ran down the stairway, unable to turn around, needing to be far away from him.

When she got to the office, she hurried to her desk, not

wanting to talk to anyone. She'd gotten another job. She'd given up her hopes to be promoted—all for Garrett. How could she have been so wrong about him?

She had believed he loved her. She'd believed he wanted them to have a life together. Why had he rented a singles apartment for two years? Why?

"Elena, I heard that Stanley's going to be okay," Grace said, startling her back to reality.

"Is he home?" she asked, relieved he was all right.

"He'll be going home tomorrow morning," the receptionist replied. "Garrett's picking him up. Will you be going with him?"

"I don't think so." She grabbed a bunch of files from her desk, unable to deal with her emotions about Garrett. "I'd better get this work done before I leave."

She hid in the file room, feeling all mixed-up inside, desperately trying to put Garrett out of her mind. She realized that now, more than ever, she couldn't continue working for Grant Property Management, not when Garrett would be there. She'd give her notice as soon as Stanley was home.

After work she drove straight to her sister's house, needing the comfort of her family's love. When she got there, Jan was barely able to say hello. She was taking Bennie's temperature. His face was red and his forehead hot. He was crying that his body hurt all over. Tod was near his brother, playing with a stuffed animal, trying to make him laugh.

"Bennie's got a hundred-and-four fever!" Jan said worriedly.

"Let's get him into a cool bath," Elena suggested.

Alone in the bathroom, as she went to fill the tub with water, she thought of Garrett and their intimate bath together on Catalina Island. She tried to push him out of her heart, but the love she felt for him kept rushing back without control.

When Bennie's temperature went down and Jan left him sleeping in his room, her sister turned to her in the kitchen.

"El, what's wrong?" she asked. "Is it Garrett?"

She nodded, trying to stay in control. "I'm not going to cry over him. I'm not." But her eyes filled with tears, anyway.

Her sister gently touched her arm. "Did Garrett break up the relationship?"

"That's just it, Jan," she choked out. "I never had a relationship with him."

"How can you say that?"

"All along he planned to stay single," she told her.

In a rush of emotion she explained about her finding out that he recently moved into a singles-only apartment in Palms.

"I don't understand," her sister said. "He signed the Marriage Connection agreement. He made a promise to—" Bennie started crying from the bedroom. "I'll just be a minute. We'll talk more about Garrett."

"No," Elena said. "I'd better get home."

"Will you be okay?"

"I'll be fine," she told her, knowing she wouldn't be fine at all.

When she returned to her apartment, she immediately noticed the message machine blinking. Somehow she knew it was Garrett. She turned on the machine, fighting her need to hear his voice.

"Elena, I know you don't want to talk to me," Garrett began on the tape. "But you never gave me a chance to explain. Can you call me when you get in?"

She automatically picked up the phone to call him,

wanting to connect with him again. As she began dialing his number, she quickly hung up.

Why are you playing the fool again? she silently asked herself. She'd given her heart, body and soul to him. She had dreamed she would be with him forever. But he'd never shared that dream. All the while he was picturing a life without her.

Though her heart tugged to be close to him, she knew she could never fall into that tender emotional trap again.

That evening at his apartment Garrett waited for Elena to call him back. But deep down, he knew she never would. He kept seeing the pain and disillusionment in her eyes. He kept hearing her call him a liar.

Her words still bore into his chest like a bullet wound. Because he hadn't lied when he'd told her that he loved her.

During the next few days at work, he tried to finish business at the Sherman Oaks office so he could move to his new position as vice president at the Santa Monica branch. Then he'd be able to see Elena and talk to her. He'd tried calling her several more times, but she would never take his call or return it.

In the morning, just as he was packing the last box to leave, Stanley called.

"Garrett, I had planned to be at the office to welcome you to your new job," Stanley said. "But the doctor said I need to rest at home."

"Don't worry," Garrett said. "When you're back at work, you'll see my face so much that you'll wish you could be home resting again." Then the thought that was pressing at his mind burst forth. "Stan, how did Elena react when you told her about my promotion?"

"Elena is leaving the company, Garrett."

He felt like he was punched in the chest. "Where is she going?"

"She was offered a better-paying job," Stanley explained. "Today's her last day. Didn't she tell you?"

His mind was reeling. "I've been so busy with the job transition."

He heard Stanley say a few more words and then hang up. He quickly carried the boxes to his car, hoping he could catch her before she left the office.

He blamed himself for Elena leaving the company. She didn't want to be around him, not only because she'd lost the promotion to him but because he'd hurt her.

He walked into the Santa Monica office, nodded to Grace and headed toward Elena's cubicle. He found her clearing out her desk drawers.

When she glanced up at him, for a second he saw that warm sparkle in her eyes. But then a shadow took its place, and she returned to her packing.

"Elena, I heard you're leaving," he said.

"That's right," she replied in a cool voice, putting papers and pens into a cardboard box.

"If you don't want to be in this office because of me," he began, "you could work at the Sherman Oaks branch."

She stopped shoving things into the box and looked at him. "I didn't give my notice because you got the promotion, Garrett," she said.

"But I thought—"

"I took the new job *before* Stanley ever made his decision." She slammed closed the top drawer. "I wish you luck, Garrett."

As she hurried out of the office, he felt her heart shut tight to him. He leaned against the partition, realizing she'd quit so they could be together. He suddenly felt like the life force had been sucked out of him.

* * *

As Elena entered the office of her new job at Drexler Property Management, she felt like she was dying inside. She hated acting cold to Garrett. She hated blocking him out of her soul. But she had to. Because seeing him made her want him all over again.

Her new boss, Peter Drexler, came over to shake her hand. "Glad to have you aboard, Elena." Then he introduced her to the staff.

She greeted her new co-workers, but her heart throbbed in her chest, missing Garrett.

She walked into her small private office. She no longer had only a cubicle with a partition. She could close her door now and have total privacy. But none of the amenities seemed to matter.

She flipped through the files of properties she'd be managing, but she kept glancing at the phone, yearning to pick up the receiver and call Garrett. She couldn't forget her dream with him. She couldn't stop thinking about how she'd seen him as her future husband. The only problem was that he hadn't seen her as his future wife.

For the next torturous week, Garrett went through the motions of his new job responsibilities. The Santa Monica office felt empty without Elena. He forced himself not to call her, even when he had the phone in his hand ready to dial her number. He knew she was involved with her new job, new people. She wanted nothing to do with him.

Then, in the morning, at his apartment, before going to work, he held the geometric-patterned tie she'd given him. He slipped the silk around his neck, aching to see her more than ever.

Instead of heading to his office, he drove directly to hers, no longer able to resist his need to talk to her.

As he entered the reception area of Drexler Property

Management, his body felt tense, knowing she might reject him again, but he had to take the chance.

"Is Elena Martin in?" he asked the curly-headed receptionist. "I'm Garrett Sims. I used to work with her at Grant Property Management."

I held her in my arms. I made love to her.

"Elena is at a commercial building that she manages," the young woman replied.

"Could you give me the address?" he asked. "I really need to see her about an old account she managed for our company."

"Sure." The receptionist wrote the street number down and handed it to him.

Within minutes Garrett was heading for the property. He knew that she might turn her back on him again. He knew that she might be ice-cold when he approached her. But he had to explain that he wasn't a liar. He had to tell her about the mistake he'd made with the Marriage Connection agreement.

More than anything, he desperately needed to be with her again.

Elena stood near the second-floor elevators, trying to listen to the electrician explain how he planned to solve a wiring problem in the building.

She mechanically nodded in response to him, but all she could think about was how much she missed Garrett. Deep down she still couldn't believe that he had never planned on having a lifelong relationship with her. She'd been so sure he felt as close to her as she felt to him.

She suddenly realized that the electrician had picked up his toolbox from the floor, ready to complete the wiring job. She heard herself mumble words about checking on him later to make sure the work was done to the owner's specifications.

Just then the elevator doors opened, and Garrett stepped out. His curly hair was still damp from his morning shower. He was wearing a navy suit, light blue shirt and the rainbow-colored geometric tie she'd given him.

As he walked in her direction, she tried to fight the powerful feelings welling up in her. Stay calm and professional, she silently told herself. But as he neared her, her heart filled with a love for him that she couldn't control.

"What're you doing here, Garrett?" she asked, trying to keep her voice steady and strong, so he wouldn't see how vulnerable she felt in his presence.

"The secretary at your office said I'd find you here," he began, and then his voice softened. "I need to talk to you, Elena."

She felt herself weakening, realizing that he'd gone out of his way to see her. She yearned to surrender to her overwhelming love for him. But her protective instincts stopped her.

There's no future with him, she silently reminded herself.

"I don't have time right now," she quickly responded. "I need to get back to work."

She blindly pressed the Down button for an elevator, wishing their relationship could be the way she wanted.

He was suddenly standing very close to her. "Won't you let me explain about my singles apartment?" he asked.

"What for?" she told him. "I already know where I stand in your life. I already know that you don't want to—"

Her voice caught. She didn't want to say *marry me*. She didn't want to look like she was imploring him to propose to her.

Seeing that the busy elevators weren't coming, she

walked past him to the exit door to the stairwell to get to the lobby.

She hurried down the steps, knowing the longer she was near him, the more she would want him. Then she'd forget that their relationship was doomed to go nowhere.

As she opened the metal door to the lobby, she felt his strong hands on her shoulders, gently whirling her around to face him.

His warm breath was against her face. His eyes were steady on hers. She yearned to be in his arms, feeling his mouth on hers. She ached to hear the words, *I'll always be with you.*

"Elena, I should have told you about my singles apartment," he began. "I should have told you that—"

"Does it matter?" she cut in. "You signed the two-year lease because our relationship meant nothing to you."

"That's not true," he protested. "I was on a waiting list for the apartment. I had already paid the security and first and last months' rent in advance. I signed the lease before I ever met you."

"You did?" she asked, a spark of hope rising within her. Maybe she hadn't been wrong about him after all. Maybe— "Then the Marriage Connection dates meant as much to you as they did to me?"

"Yes, Elena," he replied. "But I didn't enroll in the dating service myself. My aunt entered my name."

"My sister did with me, too!" she blurted, her heart singing.

"But when my aunt had me sign the contract," he went on, "I didn't know what I was getting into. The first page was missing, the one that included the name of the service and the commitment about marriage."

"Garrett," she began, unable to hold back, desperately needing to ask the question she wanted to know more than anything. "Would you sign the Marriage Connection agreement now, if you knew that marriage was the ultimate goal?"

She held her breath, waiting for the immediate yes that would seal her heart to his forever.

He hesitated, and his eyes dimmed. "Elena—"

Her heart fell, and she knew his answer loud and clear. She turned away from him, yanked open the lobby door and hurried into the lobby, not wanting to hear any more.

She didn't remember getting into her car in the underground parking garage. She sat there with the engine off, trying to contain her turbulent emotions. Maybe she should have given him more time to answer her question. Maybe if—

Stop kidding yourself! she silently screamed. *If Garrett really loved me, he would've said an immediate 'Yes, I want to marry you.'* The fact was he didn't want a lifetime together with her!

She drove out of the parking garage back to her office, feeling a dark emptiness she knew no one could ever fill but Garrett.

At his oak desk at Grant Property Management, Garrett went through the physical motions of making business calls, feeling a frustration he could barely control.

He knew he'd failed Elena because he couldn't give her the answer she wanted to hear. Yet, how could he when he still felt a lingering conflict about getting married again?

Thinking he heard Elena's voice outside his office door, he jumped out of the chair and rushed out.

"Who are you looking for, Garrett?" Grace asked.

"I thought I heard—" He stopped, noticing a female client walking into a junior manager's cubicle. "I made a mistake, Grace."

He returned to his office, realizing he'd fantasized that Elena had come back to hear him out, that she wanted to understand him. But why should she?

He had told her that he loved her. Yet he hadn't taken the next relationship step with her. Why should she waste her time with him?

Grace buzzed him. "Stanley's on the phone."

"Garrett, how does it feel sitting in the vice president's chair?" his employer asked over the line.

"Great, Stan, just great," he forced out, knowing deep down, the new position had no meaning to him without Elena in his life.

That evening, when Garrett was at baseball practice at the ball field, he immediately noticed Julie sitting in the bleachers, waiting to go to dinner with Trey after practice. He ached for Elena to be waiting for him.

Frustrated, Garrett pitched the ball with such force that pain shot through his shoulder joint. He grabbed his shoulder, unable to finish practice. Trey got ice from the soda chest.

"Garrett, stop fighting it," his friend told him. "You're miserable without Elena."

He winced as he pressed the ice to his sore shoulder. "She's never coming back," he said, the words like needles in his skin.

"Oh, yeah?" his buddy said, glancing at his wife. "If she loves you, she'll be back." He winked at Julie. "I know."

At his apartment Garrett felt like the walls were closing in on him. He couldn't eat his frozen dinner. He turned on the TV and then turned it off. He glanced out the window and saw single people entering their apartments, going home alone like he was.

He suddenly felt a loneliness he could no longer tolerate. He knew he couldn't take another month, another week, another day, living in the singles-only complex. Every moment he spent in the building reminded him of how hollow his life was without Elena.

The next day, Garrett met with the owner, Sam McGrath, and told him that he had to break the two-year lease. He knew he'd lose his security deposit and his last-month's rent money. But he didn't care. After sharing an intense love with Elena, he had no desire to live a singles-only lifestyle.

He lucked out and soon found an apartment in a family building in West Los Angeles. He was immediately welcomed by a married couple with two kids who lived in the apartment next door. He waited for an uncomfortable feeling to grip him, being around a happily married couple while he was still alone in his life, just like he'd felt after his marriage had broken up.

Instead, the closeness between the husband and wife made him think about him and Elena. And he yearned to be with her even more.

He took a chance and left another message on her answering machine, asking if he could meet with her. When she didn't respond, he knew he couldn't give up. He tried to come up with another idea for seeing her, but he didn't know what else to do.

"You blew it with Elena, didn't you?" Aunt Rosie said when he took her to visit his new apartment.

"Yeah," he admitted, unable to keep his frustration bottled up anymore.

"Do you want her back?" his aunt asked.

"More than anything," he said with all his heart.

"Then sit down and come up with a plan," she told him. "I'm not waiting a second longer to meet the perfect woman for you."

Garrett didn't know how, but he was going to see Elena. And she was definitely going to meet his aunt.

* * *

A few days later, after work Elena dropped by her apartment to get her mail. She glanced at the answering machine, but there were no messages from Garrett. She realized that he'd finally stopped calling her.

The ache in her heart was so heavy that she quickly drove to her sister's house, hoping that being with Jan and her nephews would fill the hollow in her heart that she felt without Garrett.

While Jan helped Tod and Bennie with their homework, Elena flipped through the mail she'd taken with her. When she saw an envelope from the Marriage Connection, she flashed on her prearranged dates with Garrett and how she'd fallen crazy in love with him right from the start.

In the letter, the dating service requested that a rating sheet be filled out indicating whether or not the three dates had been successful.

She squeezed the paper between her fingertips, wishing the Marriage Connection had worked for her, wishing Garrett was with her that very moment, because she still loved him so much.

"El, why don't you call him?" Jan said as she entered the kitchen.

"I can't," Elena said, putting the letter into her bag. "I just can't."

"I wish there was something I could do," her sister said helplessly.

"Don't worry, I'll get over him," she insisted. Her sister looked at her doubtfully. "I will. I really will." But she wasn't sure it was possible.

Saturday morning Elena drove to her sister's to baby-sit her nephews so Jan could go to work. She hoped playing with the kids would keep her mind off Garrett, because so far, nothing else had.

When she arrived at her sister's, she was surprised to find Jan still in her nightgown and robe. "Jan, you're going to be late for work."

"El, I'm not feeling very well this morning," her sister began. "Do you think you could cover for me at work? I don't want to lose this job."

"I don't know anything about your work," she quickly replied. "Plus, the lady you work for doesn't know me."

"I already called her," Jan went on. "She's fine about your coming over. All you need to do is clean up and do any errands she might need."

"Jan—"

"Please?"

She couldn't refuse her sister. "Okay, I'll do it," she replied, hoping that maybe doing something totally different might take her thoughts off the man she still loved.

"You're the best, El!" Jan said, hugging her.

She grabbed her bag. "What's the lady's name?"

"Rose."

That morning Garrett quickly stuffed his laundry into the apartment building washer. He hoped Elena wouldn't get angry with him for creating a plan to meet her. He had no other choice. If she refused to see him on her terms, then he'd have to see her on his.

As the washer whirred, he went over in his head a zillion times what he would say to her. But none of the words felt right to him.

He needed her to know how much he loved her, how much he missed her and how his life was a total void without her. He couldn't allow himself to think that maybe she no longer wanted to be with him. He couldn't emotionally deal with that option at all.

Before he knew it, the wash cycle ended. He opened

the lid and took out his wet clothes to put into the dryer, when he saw that all of his white cotton briefs were pink!

He realized he was so nervous about seeing Elena that he'd accidentally put his scarlet-colored baseball jersey into the white wash!

Elena knocked on the front door of the address that her sister had given her. The door opened, and an elderly woman with bright eyes and gray hair, a bit mussed, stared at her.

"I'm Jan's sister."

"Yes, come in, come in," the woman said. "I was just putting away some clothes in my bedroom."

Elena stepped into the small house. The sofa and chairs were upholstered in flowered fabric. There was a stack of newspapers next to a lounge chair. The radio was set to the soft-beat radio station that her sister listened to.

She realized that helping Jan wasn't making her forget about Garrett at all. Maybe she should call him. Maybe he'd changed his mind about his future. She knew she was thinking crazy, but she couldn't help it. She wanted to be with him so much.

"My bedroom is in here," the elderly woman said as she led her into a room with a canopied bed.

Dresses and empty hangers were strewn on the unmade bed. The woman began picking up a dress to hang.

"I'll do that for you," Elena said.

"Oh, thank you," the lady said. "Your sister is a whiz at taking care of everything. I was lucky to find her."

"Jan's great," she agreed.

Elena was about to hang up the dress when her eye caught a photograph on the dresser. She walked over as if in a daze and picked up the frame to look more closely at the photo. The curly black hair. The sexy charcoal eyes. It was Garrett!

"Handsome man, isn't he?" the woman said. "Garrett's my nephew. I raised him as if he were my own son."

Elena stared at her. "*You're* Aunt Rosie?" she asked, flabbergasted.

"Yup," she replied. "And you're the young lady my nephew's in love with."

Her mind was whirling. "I—I don't understand."

"It's really quite simple." Rose headed into the living room as Elena followed, totally confused.

"A few days ago, while your sister was here, I was listening to a dating service advertisement on the radio," Rose explained. "The 'something' connection."

"Marriage Connection?" she asked, her breathing quickening with anticipation.

"Yes, that's it," the old woman replied as she sat in the lounge chair. "Jan and I realized that my nephew and her sister had been matched by the service."

"Jan knows that you're Garrett's aunt?" She sat down in shock, her thoughts traveling light speed through her brain. "Then my sister wasn't really sick this morning. You and she—"

"—plotted to get you here," Rose finished for her. "Sometimes family needs to intervene when a couple is having trouble with their future plans."

"But Garrett doesn't want a future with me," she blurted.

"You're wrong, Elena." Rose leaned forward and took her hands in hers. "My nephew is wildly in love with you. He talks about you all the time. He's miserable that you won't see him."

"I want to," she admitted. "But I can't. I want a husband, but he doesn't want a wife."

"Nonsense," she told her. "My nephew would propose

to you in a second if he wasn't so scared of getting married again.''

"*Again?*" she repeated, stunned. "Garrett never told me that he was married before."

"My nephew has a lot of pride—too much sometimes," Rose said. "He doesn't like to talk about that marriage because he got severely burned by his ex-wife."

She felt a sudden pain in her chest thinking that someone had hurt him. "What did she do to him?"

"The little lady conned him out of all his money," Rose replied, "and then she ran off with another man."

"Oh, no," she whispered, realizing the unbearable pain he must've gone through. Now she knew why he was hesitant to get married again. She couldn't blame him for wanting to stay single after what that woman did to him. Yet she knew that if she was Garrett's wife, she never would leave him, not ever.

"Aunt Rosie!" Garrett's voice called out from the other room as the back door opened.

Her pulse raced. Her hands grew moist. Her eyes anxiously darted to Rose.

"I'm in the living room," Rose said with a pleased smile on her face.

When Garrett walked in, a streak of heat rushed through her bloodstream. She wanted to jump up from the sofa and run into his arms. But she couldn't, because she wasn't sure at all if he was ready for a long-term relationship with her.

"It's time for my late-morning nap," Rose said, arising from her chair. "Elena, I appreciate your coming over. Say hello to your sister for me."

"Don't you need me for anything else?" Elena quickly asked, anxious about being alone with Garrett, knowing how much she loved and wanted him.

"You came for exactly the reason I needed," the

woman replied, giving a mischievous wink to her nephew, as though their plan was working perfectly. Then she disappeared into her bedroom and closed the door.

"Elena, don't be mad at me for coming over like this," he said. "But I had to see you." His warm eyes held hers, and she couldn't help melting inside. "I miss you, Elena. I miss you so much."

She wanted him to hold her. She wanted him to kiss her, but she couldn't give in to her feelings until she was sure.

"I miss you, too, Garrett," she admitted. "But we have different goals for the future. Your aunt told me about your past marriage. I understand why you don't want to get married again."

"But I do."

"But you said—"

He moved close to her as though he wanted to touch her but didn't dare. "Elena, I love you more than any woman I've ever known," he said. "I've fantasized about marrying you."

"You have?" she asked, filled with hope.

"So many times," he said. "But I don't want a temporary marriage this time."

Her heart burst with love for him. She wanted to tell him, *I'll always be with you, Garrett!* But how could she totally trust that he had no more doubts about being with her forever?

"I want to be with you, Garrett," she said. "But how can I be sure that you're ready to make an eternal commitment?"

"I'll prove it," he said. "There is one more Marriage Connection date on the contract, written in small print."

"There is?" she asked, her heart palpitating with anticipation.

"Will you go on that date with me right now?" he asked, his voice rising with hope.

"Yes, I'll go!" she replied, unable to say it fast enough.

Sitting next to Garrett in his Mustang, Elena tried to contain her excitement that maybe her dream would come true with him.

"Where is our date?" she couldn't help but ask.

"At my apartment."

Then, instead of driving to Palms, he parked his car in front of a residential building in West Los Angeles.

"Here we are," he said, opening the passenger door for her.

"I thought we were going to your singles-only apartment."

"I broke the lease," he replied, taking her hand in his.

"You did?" she asked. "You really did?"

He nodded, squeezing her hand. He led her down a hallway past open apartment doors where she saw children playing and elderly couples watching television together.

She glanced at Garrett, who was watching her with warm eyes, and she knew that he had left his apartment because of her.

The moment she entered his living room, she saw the geometric-patterned tie she'd given him lying across the back of the sofa, as though she was still very much a part of his life.

"Do you like my new place?" he asked.

"I love it!" she burst out.

As she checked out the kitchen, she suddenly stopped. Lying on the table was a petite silver-wrapped box with her name on the gift tag. Before she could catch her breath, her gaze immediately landed on something else.

Next to the silver box was the first page of the Marriage Connection agreement. Highlighted in neon green was the sentence that she never thought he'd ever agree to. "The only requirement is a commitment to want to get married." And underneath, scribbled in dark blue ink, was Garrett's signature agreeing to the marriage requirement.

Tears filled her eyes. "Garrett, are you sure?" she asked. "Are you really sure?"

"I'm very sure," he replied, handing her the silver box.

When she opened it, her breath caught when she saw the dazzling pear-shaped diamond engagement ring inside.

"Elena, will you be my wife for always?" he asked, his voice filled with emotion.

"Garrett, I can't imagine my life without you!" she burst out.

As he slipped the white gold on her finger, he whispered, "I love you so much, Elena."

She immediately went into his arms and whispered against his lips, "I'll always be with you, Garrett, always."

Feeling ecstatically happy and so very lucky that he was her man, Elena couldn't help silently thanking the Marriage Connection for matching her with the perfect man, Garrett Sims, who made a commitment to be her husband forever!

* * * * *

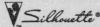